THE NAKED MADONNA

JAN WIESE is a distinguished book publisher, for many years Managing Director of a leading Oslo publishing house, Cappelens, and chairman of the Norwegian Publishers' Association. This his first novel has been acquired for publication in a number of foreign editions.

First published in Norway with the title
Kvinnen som kledte seg naken for sin elskede
by Gyldendal Norsk Forlag, Oslo, 1990

First published in Great Britain, 1995
by The Harvill Press
84 Thornhill Road
London N1 1RD

First impression

© 1990 Gyldendal Norsk Forlag
English translation © The Harvill Press 1995

Jan Wiese asserts the moral right to be
identified as the author of this work.

A CIP catalogue record for this book
is available from the British Library.

This translation has been published with
the financial support of NORLA.

ISBN 1 86046 024 0 hardback
1 86046 025 9 paperback

Photoset in Monophoto Bembo
by Servis Filmsetting Limited, Manchester

Printed and bound in Great Britain by
Butler & Tanner Ltd, Frome and London

THE NAKED
MADONNA

Jan Wiese

*Translated from the Norwegian
by Tom Geddes*

The Harvill Press

CONTENTS

ROME 1989

The Age of Miracles is Past

The graffiti scowl at me with their virulent yellow fluorescent lettering on the wall. I see them every morning when I go over to the window and watch the daily bustle outside.

There's probably something in it.

There's been a strained relationship between God and man for a long time.

This week's newspapers carried the report of its final termination, the very last message from God. From now on no more signs can be expected.

He has turned His back on mankind. Or can it be that in reality He has never existed? Not as anything more than a myth, looked up to for thousands of years by a mankind desperate to believe. Have all the messages throughout the whole of that time just been a recurrent dream within ourselves? Can it be that He has only lived in our belief?

But if God is only a myth, existence must nevertheless be controlled by something, by a superior structured providence without a soul. I occasionally incline to such a concept. Yet I would rather believe that God does exist, but that He has become weary. He no longer wants to hold His hand over the people that He once created in His own image.

There are reports in the newspapers of the catastrophe that occurred on Sunday, 3rd September 1989. During the

3

consecration of the new church in Perugia the whole building suddenly collapsed and crushed all of the seven hundred or more people who were there for the service.

So far only one person has been rescued from the ruins, and there is little hope of finding any more. Among the dead are a number of prominent representatives of church and state: cardinals and bishops, several cabinet ministers and many guests from ecclesiastical and cultural circles throughout Europe.

The newspapers are full of the incomprehensible disaster; even yesterday's football league match has been given less space than usual. The catastrophe is examined from all angles:

Who is among the dead?

How could anything like this happen? Was there a fault in the construction of the new building?

Everyone seems to think so, and veiled hints at the architect's guilt, though tentative for the moment, are clear enough. He himself has no chance of defending himself, he's lying buried beneath the rubble of the walls along with all the others.

The new church in Perugia has been a centre of attention for several years. The media have been obsessed with it ever since the foundation stone was laid. There have been television and newspaper reports on it over and over again. The underlying assumption was that the new project represented a ray of hope, a desperate wish to reconstruct a relationship with God.

The creator of this church is, or rather was, the new architectural genius, a well-known personality in all the media. His face has been appearing everywhere, on the screen as well as in the newspapers, particularly after he won the competition for the church in Perugia. In interviews he has been explaining his desire to build the church to re-establish contact between God and mankind. It would be a confirmation of God's love for us and our faith in Him.

4

He had nonchalantly taken upon himself the role of God's interpreter and messenger. I can still see his face in front of me in a television interview explaining his intentions: the object of such soaring arches was to imbue the construction with a deeper, religious significance. To me he seemed arrogant, even hubristic.

It is all being reported again now, after the terrible disaster.

The church at Perugia was very modern in design. Even when it was still on the drawing board there were many protests from older people who thought it didn't look like a house of God. There was widespread discussion in the press for some time. Meanwhile, the church took shape, and there was general agreement in one respect at least: that it was something very special. Eventually, most concurred with the view that the architect had effected a renewal of church architecture with a touch of genius, he had created vaulted arches which seemed in their daring to surpass the bounds of the possible.

The prison warder is bringing in my meal, and I raise my eyes momentarily from the newspaper reports. Has he read them? His only reaction to the catastrophe is a shrug of the shoulders. We're too far away from Perugia and besides he doesn't know anyone there. He goes out through the cell door again and closes it after him.

I take a sip of the weak, boiling-hot coffee. The front page of *Il Popolo* shouts at me with its gigantic lettering. One person escaped alive from the whole thing, the newspaper has interviewed him, see page six.

The man who was saved is a young craftsman, a carpenter. He's in a state of shock, that's quite evident from the journalist's report.

My own eyes begin to open wider.

What the young man has to say makes my heart beat faster.

He tells of the church filling to capacity with an expectant crowd quite early in the morning. He himself had diffidently pushed his way through the door furthest from the altar.

There was still an hour to go before the service was due to begin. From where he was standing, a picture on the wall caught his eye, a painting of the Virgin Mary with the Child in her arms. He felt as if the woman in the painting was staring at him and holding his gaze, and he noticed that despite the crush the atmosphere in the church had become quite solemn during this long period of waiting.

But it was only when the procession of clergy had finally entered and made its way up the aisle that, according to the young man, something strange happened.

All at once, without any signal, the congregation stood up and began to sing. He realised with astonishment that he was singing too; he knew the words even though he didn't understand them. They were in Latin and it sounded like an ancient hymn. It began almost as a whisper, but the alien words soon rose in a crescendo of sound.

The singing filled the church, and suddenly he could see the sound waves vibrating. They became increasingly concentrated until they merged into one, and at that very moment the air seemed to explode. In desperation he kept his eyes fixed on the Madonna.

He noticed that everything stood still for one brief instant, before the walls started to shake and crumble. It was all over in a matter of seconds, the church was in total ruins, and seven hundred people lay buried underneath. He himself had escaped, as if by a miracle. He had woken up on the grassy slope beyond the piles of rubble. Everything was silent.

The doctors at the hospital where the man was taken confirm that this sole eyewitness emerged from the disaster with his hearing completely destroyed, but otherwise free from physical injury.

But it was emphasised that he was still in a state of shock.

I search agitatedly further through the columns. There's nothing more about the painting.

6

It must have been about a year earlier that I'd found the wondrous painting of Mary and the Child, in the Vatican. After a lot of argument it was decided that the picture would be donated to the church in Perugia. The ecclesiastical authorities in the Vatican wished to make their gift to the new church and at the same time to affirm the continuity of the Catholic Church, the old in the new.

The new church building was also itself a gift, a donation from a very rich banker who wanted to ensure his posthumous renown. Evil tongues maintained that he had already done that, since he had made his fortune in ways that wouldn't stand up to scrutiny. His contacts with the Mafia were well known to those who took an interest in such liaisons. Church leaders, however, turned a deaf ear to any gossip of that kind.

The Vatican's intention was for the painting to serve as the altarpiece for the church, but the architect protested. The venerable painting would clash with the modernity of the church. The new altarpiece was already made, a stylised white dove in flight. So it was decided that the painting, probably by an unknown artist in the fifteenth century, should hang instead in one of the transepts.

Only in the next day's paper have I at last found what I've been searching for. A signed article in *Il Messaggero* says that the painting was totally destroyed along with everything else when the church collapsed. The name of the journalist stares out at me, the same one who covered the news of the murder last autumn.

I know more about this than the newspapers report. If the truth be told, I am myself a small part of the story. It includes *my* tragedy too. So I have decided to use the coming days to assemble what I know, and recount the whole as I have experienced it. Not being believed has been hard to bear.

If I'm going to do that, I'll also have to say something about myself. That's complete anathema to me, I've never liked any kind of examination of my own character. I regard myself as a somewhat boring research worker without a glimmer of what nowadays is called "charisma".

My father had disappeared from my life before I was born, and my mother died when I was seven. She was always angry when she spoke of my father, and that's perhaps why I remember it so well. According to her he was an incorrigible fantasiser and a failed inventor. The only thing I have of his is a briefcase containing a hundred copies of patent applications, and clipped to every one of them is a formal letter from the Patent Office advising him that the application has been considered and rejected.

The hundredth and final application is for an invention to make rain. It states that it is based on an ancient design that he inherited from his father. It's dated 4th August 1935.

I was conceived on the same day. My father must have been so excited about his latest application that he managed to talk my mother away from the bookshop where she worked and right into bed. He had flirted with her before from time to time when he was in the shop. But, according to my mother, that day was the first and last occasion they were properly together. She was ignoring two hours at the end of September. That was when they got married, the same day that my father was sent to Ethiopia and the war.

There's not much more to say about my father. He deserted.

He was sitting in camp one day with his mates eating dinner. He was expatiating on a new invention he'd made that would revolutionise the world. Suddenly he fell silent right in the middle of a sentence and a faraway expression came into his eyes. He stood up and walked straight out of the camp without looking back. He has never been seen since.

I am fifty-three and a librarian by profession. I've been attached to the manuscript collections in the Vatican for twenty long years, the last two as head of research. If I'm to do myself justice, I have to say that I've built up a certain reputation over the years as an expert on older manuscripts. I won respect in academic circles with my thesis on St Pachomius' *Rules* from the fourth century.

I have literally buried myself in manuscripts. All these documents live their own lives, and in a strange way they have also taken hold of my life and assumed control over it.

Now in retrospect it feels as if I was released for a short period when I met the woman who became my wife. She was sixteen years younger than I was. I had reconciled myself by that time to the idea of living alone for the rest of my days; working with manuscripts filled my life and gave it meaning. And ever since my youth I have suffered from a troublesome shyness, especially with regard to women, a feeling that has undoubtedly been increased by my rather solitary and absorbing work.

I met her for the first time at a press conference in the Sheraton Hotel, organised by Mondadori. They had published a de luxe edition of a mediaeval manuscript in facsimile. I had written an article about the manuscript a few years earlier, and I had now been invited to write a foreword to the new edition. I was introduced to the journalists at the press conference as the expert who would be answering their questions. It was an unusual situation for me, and I felt embarrassed, as so often before.

It was then that I caught the eye of a young woman just in front of me. She smiled and her gaze was unwavering. I felt happy and was suddenly able to find the right words.

Afterwards there were canapés and white wine. The woman came over and introduced herself. She represented the advertising agency that the publishing house was using for the launch. I soon discovered that she *was* the little agency that she herself, despite her youth, had started and for which she had won considerable respect.

9

I managed of course to spill wine on her dress in a clumsy attempt to shake hands while at the same time balancing a glass and plate. She brushed aside my stuttering excuses with a smile and was quite unperturbed.

She rang me the next day, wanting some more information about the manuscript. We had lunch together and I could feel an unsettling *frisson* between us.

We met quite often in the weeks that followed. Eventually we went to the theatre together and to a few concerts. The latter was her idea; I'm fairly unmusical myself. But my interest was so aroused by that time that I dared not admit my lack of talent.

In the concert hall I felt an increasing delight in just sitting close to her. But even in situations like that I never had the courage to take her hand. I was and remained shy. A cautious kiss on the cheek when we met or said goodbye was for a long time our only physical contact. Until one day she invited me back for dinner.

She lived in a modern, expensive apartment, quite centrally situated. The furnishing and decoration gave evidence of confident taste; I remember thinking that this was how a person in advertising lives.

I wasn't exactly enthusiastic. I was happiest in my old den, full of books and shabby furniture. But I didn't say so.

She was good at cooking too, and at creating a relaxed atmosphere around her.

After dinner we sat drinking a glass of wine together; I was cursing my ineptitude, but still could not overcome my bashfulness.

It was then that she got up. A determined look came over her, and without a word she undressed right before my very eyes.

She stood in front of me and looked me straight in the face.

Afterwards I could no longer understand my own shyness.

I got used to being naked surprisingly quickly, and to being close to her nakedness. But when we'd got to that point, she herself was suddenly not so self-assured. She blushed and lowered her eyes and hid her face. It would confuse me again and again, this abrupt shift from resolute woman to timid, innocent girl.

From then on we were inseparable, even though we each kept our own apartment for almost a year. Despite that we never slept apart for a single night. This period was probably the happiest of all in our short life together.

Nevertheless it was far from practical having two places to live. I never brought up the problem myself, because I took it for granted that she wouldn't want to give up her modern comforts, while I for my part was unwilling to relinquish my own little slum.

Once more, it was she who took the initiative. She would sell her apartment and move in with me. I was both pleased and surprised. But that night I lay awake after she had gone to sleep and went over everything in my mind. Would this be for the best? Would it be possible for her to settle down in my dilapidated, unpractical old flat?

The next morning I suggested that we could carry on living in her apartment, but that I could perhaps furnish one room with my things as a study. I could tell how happy she was when she threw her arms around my neck.

A month later we were married.

We were very different, but I think I can say that we lived together in perfect harmony for five years. I'm very quiet by nature myself, fairly taciturn, but on the other hand a good listener. Books mean a lot to me in life, as do the manuscripts in the Vatican. They fill the working day and as often as not all my free time. I like being at home best, and am not keen on being among people. In fact I've discovered that I even rather enjoy being in my prison cell.

My wife was quite the opposite. She was a tall, elegant woman, cheerful and very vivacious. And above all, she was pretty. I never understood why she had taken an interest in an oddball like me. But she had. I believed her when she constantly told me that she loved me.

She was obviously capable and immensely hard-working, and I think she ran the advertising agency very well. She started early and worked late, and she was always out somewhere, even in the evenings, at meetings and receptions. Because of the agency she had to keep up a wide range of contacts in the business.

At the beginning I went to several such gatherings with her, but fairly soon we came to an unspoken agreement that she would go alone, while I stayed at home with my books.

I actually knew very little about the office and her work there. I tried to ask questions and get some impression of the way she spent her days, but she had the knack of turning the conversation on to other subjects without making it obvious that she was doing so.

She could talk about anything, people, books, politics, music, and eventually even about my manuscripts. She insisted on knowing what I was doing, and she had an amazing ability to familiarise herself with anything new. I soon discovered that with her practical and effective approach, allied to a lively imagination, she could give me surprising new insights into the problems I was dealing with.

She was always happy to come back home to me, and I loved her.

I have been continuing my scholarly work here in prison. At least my superiors in the Vatican didn't cut off my hand after the terrible event. Every morning at nine a messenger from the library delivers a portfolio containing the manuscripts that I'm studying at the moment. At five o'clock he is there again to take the material back.

The messenger first turned up the very week after sentence was passed. I was still in such a state of despair that I couldn't bring myself to look at the papers.

After a while my interest was rekindled. I was soon immersed in the old manuscripts once again. Eventually I began submitting a list of the documents I wanted the following morning.

One day, a Thursday, the messenger brought two cartons. Besides the usual one containing manuscripts, there was a box with three bottles of wine in it, of a quite exceptional quality. After that a box of three bottles arrived every Thursday. And inside was a card bearing greetings from the Cardinal.

I'm working well, and I must also admit that I'm enjoying the superb wine. But don't think for a moment that I've forgotten why I'm here. How can I ever forget that?

Long before I received the first consignment of wine I'd thought that I should write down my story and bring the pieces of the puzzle together.

I have put off commencing it, primarily because I know it will be painful to relive everything. But also because I want to read again the particular documents I was studying in the days leading up to my breakdown. They provide the key to everything that has happened. I've been trying to get them delivered, but every time I find they've been deleted from the list.

It's not so surprising. Even during the trial the Vatican denied all knowledge of them. The Cardinal declared under oath that neither he nor anyone else in the library had ever seen or heard of the manuscripts I was demanding, and that I insisted would be of the greatest interest for the case.

I believed him then. It wasn't so strange. I was the one who discovered the documents; I didn't show them to anyone, but took them home to read. When I travelled up to the north to look for the dagger, they were on my desk. But no one has seen them since. They have vanished without trace.

It was after the Cardinal started sending me the wine in prison that I began to suspect the Vatican's good faith.

As time has passed I've had an increasing conviction that someone from the library must have come to the apartment and taken the documents away. Doubtless they're safely back in the archives.

The Cardinal sent the wine just to divert me from my purpose. He thought I would distract the faithful in their search for God.

After the dreadful catastrophe in Perugia I have decided. On today's "order form" I have again asked for the documents to be sent. The Cardinal can't prevent it any longer. He himself was among the dead in Sunday's disaster.

And if they still persist in refusing me the manuscripts, I have fortunately kept the detailed notes from the last time I read them. I can reproduce their contents with a good degree of accuracy. I can also more easily present the whole thing in a readable Italian; the old Latin was rather stilted and in parts difficult to interpret.

Singing Valley

Not far from the town of La Spezia, on the Ligurian Sea, there is a little village hidden between the mountains. It bears the resonant name of Singing Valley. There are very few people living there today; no one wants to live in such inaccessible places any more. The road, or rather track, that leads to it follows steep mountain sides and almost impenetrable defiles. At some points it gives the impression of hanging in midair.

It's possible to take a car for the first few kilometres, then the track gets so narrow that only those familiar with it can guide a horse very cautiously over the mountains and down into the isolated valley. It has always taken three days for a traveller to make his way from the coast, through the jagged mountain passes, to those black-clad people.

In fact the path continues further; it has wound its way since time immemorial through the village in the valley and on eastwards, until it emerges on the road to Prato.

Nowadays, as in bygone ages, it's just those with business in Singing Valley who use the tortuous track. Those who have no other choice. In other words, the only people who pass that way are the valley's own inhabitants carrying goods by pack-horse to and from the village between the mountains.

The valley has long been known for its red wine. The vines grow in the thin soil up the steep valley sides. The wine from the area has a taste of its own, quite unlike wine from the other districts in Liguria. As everyone knows, the wines from this region have all lost their individuality and are blended into a unified quality, DOC Cinqueterra, a dry wine best drunk locally.

The wine from Singing Valley, on the other hand, is unknown to ordinary people today. It is never exported, nor is it ever sold in shops here in Italy. The production isn't great, but nevertheless substantial enough for many to wonder where it makes its way after it's carried to the coast on horseback in skins.

The truth is that it's sent on to Rome, more precisely to the Vatican State, where it's bottled, labelled, and stored in cellars.

The label was drawn by a well-known artist around the turn of the century. It's a picture of a church between mountains in Art Nouveau style.

Only after many years' maturation does the wine reach the table of the higher echelons of the prelates and officers of the Vatican. It has been extolled by them for almost two hundred years as a gift from God.

That's how long the Vatican has had a standing order for the purchase of all the wine from the valley. I've checked back in the Vatican account book myself, and according to those the first wine bought from Singing Valley arrived in 1809.

But I've also discovered that there was a delivery of wine sent the year before, as a present from the then Bishop of La Spezia.

In the books where all the donations to the Vatican are carefully recorded, there's a note of receipt from the Bishop of a gift of a painting of the Holy Virgin and Child together with six dozen skins of wine. Accompanying the delivery was a letter from the Bishop dated 3rd May 1808 in Singing Valley. For both the painting and the wine the register is annotated: *Source unknown.*

It was many years ago when I discovered where the special wine came from. As I've mentioned, I've worked as a researcher in the manuscripts department of the Vatican for two decades. I remember in my very first week in the library being called in to see the Cardinal in charge of manuscripts. He was a friendly prelate who offered me a glass of wine; that was the first time I sampled the red wine from Singing Valley. He also told me the story of the Bishop who had donated both the painting and the wine.

"He probably wanted to exert influence before a new Cardinal was chosen. And he succeeded too: barely a month later he was selected."

I should have asked a number of questions on that very first occasion, of course. But, excited at being given wine by a Cardinal, I listened solemnly to his tale. The wine had found such favour that the decision-makers in the Vatican had placed an order for all the future production from the valley.

I have since discovered that this wine marks a social distinction in the Vatican, between those who have access to it and those who don't. It took two decades of service before I was deemed worthy myself. I'm not a theologian, but a librarian by training. I was eventually appointed head of research, with responsibility for a special little department in the immense manuscript archives.

When I accepted the promotion, two years ago, I had an audience with the Cardinal again, a successor to the one I'd met before. Once more the red wine appeared on the table, the same kind that I've been given subsequently on very rare occasions over the years. He congratulated me on my new post, and mentioned in passing that I could now buy the wine myself from the Vatican wineshop.

I should mention that I had tried to get it before, but in vain.

Later the same day I took two bottles home with me to celebrate the appointment that I'd been half hoping for and half expecting for several years. As I poured out the wine at dinner I told my wife about its history.

She took a delicate sip from the glass, held the wine in her mouth and rolled it around her palate; she was silent for a moment, then she looked at me and asked:

"Where is the painting hanging?"

It wasn't very difficult to find it. Even if their origin is uncertain, all works of art in the Vatican are carefully catalogued, with a note of their location.

The catalogue indicated that the painting was hung in a passageway joining two of the Vatican buildings. When I went to look for it, the passage was no longer there. An inspection of older plans of the Vatican and a talk with the architects' office revealed that the passage was indeed still there, but that the door to it had been panelled over during building alterations in the previous century.

Two days later I had obtained permission, and I got help from the buildings department to remove the panel. Thus it was that the door was reopened for the first time in more than a hundred years. The little passage appeared as a long dark cavern. Whatever was hanging there would hardly ever have been noticed, even in the days when the passage was a short cut between offices. It had no window and must also have been without lighting. It had been sealed up before the age of electricity.

I shone a torch around the walls. There were several paintings hanging there, all covered in a thick layer of dust. I went slowly from picture to picture shining the torch on each one. Only by brushing away some of the dust was it possible to make out the subjects of the paintings.

When I finally came to a halt and knew that I had found the one I was searching for, I was at first disappointed. It seemed dull and flat, lifeless. For a moment or two I was tempted to let it remain there. But why would the Bishop have sent an indifferent painting as a gift if he had really wanted to make an impression on someone?

I lifted the picture carefully down from the wall and carried it out into the light. The surface of the painting was coarse and matt. I blew away most of the dust, and immediately became aware of greater depth and more colour.

In some excitement I followed along as they took the painting over to the Vatican restoration workshop, where a continuous programme of preservation of works of art goes on. I knew one of the conservators well. I stood the painting up in front of him expectantly, without saying anything, and I saw how quickly his interest was aroused.

He cautiously began to wash away the dirt in one little corner. Then, somewhat disconcerted, he picked up the painting, turned it round and looked for a distinguishing mark, but in vain. It bore no signature.

"I'll phone you," he said, "when I've cleaned it. It might take a few days."

It was a very elated conservator who rang me the next week. I dropped what I was doing and hurried over to his department. The cleaned painting was leaning against a wall on top of his workbench. He confirmed what I could see for myself:

"A masterpiece, undated and unsigned."

Overwhelmed, we sat down before the painting. The cleaning process had conjured up an almost unbelievable sight.

I am no connoisseur of art, just an interested observer who enjoys wandering around the Vatican's art collections in his lunch hour. But now I was in no doubt, in front of us was a Madonna and Child, painted as we'd never seen it before: alive and yet sublime, eyes full of purity, but at the same time a visage of experience and sorrow. A female figure more exciting than any we had previously seen painted. The picture filled us immediately with a feeling that could only be described as pious respect.

Who could have painted it? Even the conservator, who is an expert on religious art, had to give up. Even he had never seen anything like it. The composition, the perspective, the colours, the brush strokes, all evinced the work of a master, but he remained nameless. The only thing the conservator felt able to say with any certainty was that it must have been painted after the time of Giotto.

So we sought help from the Vatican's most expert art specialist, who had honorary doctorates from a number of universities. He received us irritably and not a little unwillingly when we took the painting to him. It was obviously not the first time someone had brought him a picture from the enormous collections of the Vatican for his judgement.

The conservator had wrapped the painting in paper, and we watched the famous expert's face eagerly as he unpacked it. His reaction too was clear to see.

Irritability gave way to an astonishment which soon turned into rapturous enthusiasm. Now the Roman temperament displayed itself. This short, thickset man suddenly became a bundle of energy, he veritably spoke with his body. His gestures were forceful and animated. His eyes fixed firmly on the person he was addressing, and his mobile features were full of expression.

"Give me a few days. For the moment I'm just bewildered. But there must be a clue, a context to place the painting in. It's here, and it's a masterpiece; there must be an explanation. Unfortunately it's totally unfamiliar to me and only serves to expose the gaps in my own knowledge."

The rapture had turned into anxiety; he seemed to be searching through everything he knew without finding an answer. A disturbing experience for an expert who had long been proclaimed omniscient by the knowledgeable art world.

"This painting is completely unknown to me," he mused, "and yet I have a strange feeling I've seen it before."

He took hold of it again and scrutinised it minutely, shaking his head.

He had forgotten us.

*

When we returned a week later as arranged, we found an expert who had overcome his discomfiture at his own failure of knowledge.

He freely admitted, his elation almost bursting through his general enthusiasm, that he was still unable to name the artist. And not only that: he was in the greatest doubt about period and style.

"Its age can be determined by X-ray examinations, but that will take a while," he said.

He stood by his immediate judgement: the picture was painted by a master. But all masters had their particular techniques that identified them from one painting to another. Here we were confronted by a picture without any such characteristic signs to support an attribution.

"You are undoubtedly correct in your assumption that it was painted after Giotto's time," he nodded in recognition to the conservator, who blushed slightly.

The doctor cleared his throat. We knew what was coming. He was known and loved for countless television lectures on the many art treasures of the Vatican, and his strength lay not least in his ability to find the words to describe a painting's qualities. Sometimes you might be forgiven for wondering where those qualities ended and the expert's imagination took over. He took a delight in his own eloquence, but that was exactly what made him such a favourite with his audiences.

"I actually don't know very much," he said. "I have a feeling that the Madonna and Child of the picture may have been painted in the fifteenth century.

"But to my own professional embarrassment I also incline to the opinion that the background of the picture could have been painted at the end of the nineteenth century, by the Impressionists. And then, even worse, I have to assert that the Madonna and the background must have been painted at the same time.

"The picture is painted in tempera, of the type in use five

or six hundred years ago. It has also been glued together in three pieces the way they used to make them at that period. I'm fairly certain that this is not a case of forgery perpetrated in a later age. When anything of that sort is attempted, we're always confronted by imitations of the works of known artists. That's what makes money.

"Here, on the contrary, we see a picture by an unknown painter, a genius who has not had the slightest influence on his contemporaries or successors up to now, quite simply because his talent has been hidden from the world. If the picture had been known from the time when it was completed, it would have revolutionised the art of painting as only very few works have in the course of history.

"This picture unites both tradition and revolution in the history of art. The painter has given the figures life and movement in a manner that bears witness to Giotto, and the bodies of the Madonna and Child have a fullness which is created, as in his case, by the effects of light and shade. Similarly, the distribution of colour and the composition show a striking and distinct harmony in this part of the picture. Thus far I would be certain in my judgement that it was painted some time in the fifteenth century.

"But the fact is that the rest of the painting completely contradicts any such conclusions.

"The areas around the figures and, above all, the background anticipate developments in painting by hundreds of years, right up to the end of the last century. The picture is not painted according to the window principle, with the linear perspective developed by our own Italian artists at the beginning of the fifteenth century. Rather, it bears the stamp of Impressionism in its truncated treatment of subjects, in its shimmering brush strokes and splashes of colour that tend to dissolve external reality. There is no longer a neutral background, which in Giotto's time would have been ochre or blue.

"The most surprising aspect, however, is the fact that the totally disparate styles of the painting do not have a destructive effect on the unity of the composition. They fuse together into an exciting whole. In that respect something has been created that later painters have never developed. So even today the picture has an essentially new quality to offer art and artists.

"If I try to see it in the way I imagine altarpieces were perceived more than five hundred years ago, then the pure figures of Mary and her Child immediately strike the eye. They glow with a radiant purity. But at the same time there is a fateful aura of misfortune around the figure of Mary.

"As soon as you recognise that, your attention is inexorably drawn to the surroundings. They emphasise precisely this infinite purity of the figures, not by supplementary description, but through the shock-like scream of contrast.

"The background is anything but a neutral surface. It is the painter's masterly touch to have used it to create the opposite of goodness: evil. The varying points of colour and the shimmering brush strokes illustrate the eternal confusion between man's two innate powers.

"It is painted with an intensity that reveals deep personal commitment. Anyone who can paint the evil in mankind in such a way as this must have personal experience. Because he has simultaneously preserved, in the figure of Mary, faith's vision of the good, he has been able to create an entity, a brilliant depiction of the two inseparable sides of mankind, the good and the evil.

"But I still do not know who painted it. If I'm to be honest, my strongest inclination is to turn to my own faith and contend that the painting bears the signature of God Himself."

The famous historian was silent for a moment, but without taking his eyes off the painting. Then he continued:

"Do you remember I had a feeling of having seen it before?

That was a red herring, but nevertheless of interest, because it brings us right to the beginnings of Impressionism.

"Edouard Manet painted a picture in 1882 entitled *The Bar at the Folies Bergères*. It's now in the Courtauld Gallery in London. On first glance the painting is a portrait of a girl at a bar counter, standing alone with a melancholy expression on her face. Then you notice the background, a mirror behind the bar covering four-fifths of the surface of the painting.

"Reflected in that is a glittering picture of nightclub life as a one-dimensional contrast to the sad barmaid. It was that striking revelation of two worlds in one that aroused a kind of recognition in me. I think there is more than a vague similarity between this Mary and Manet's barmaid. They are in a sense related."

Once again there was silence.

"It has happened before that an artist has remained unknown," he went on, "but never before to emerge again as a genius on a par with the very greatest. Let us assume that the picture was painted five, or at most six centuries ago.

"It would be almost unbelievable that no knowledgeable person had ever cast an evaluative eye over it in all that time. We can ignore the two hundred years in the Vatican, anything can disappear here. But where was the painting hanging for all the years before that?

"And why aren't there more paintings with the characteristics of this master? Whoever painted this must have been in a state of eruptive energy. That is to say, he must have been at a very creative period of his life. In which case, where are all his pictures, and why wasn't he known either within or beyond his own circles?

"I stand here with only one rational explanation. The artist made his breakthrough with this very painting. The emotional, almost explosive commitment he has put into it suggests that that is the case. A traumatic experience can release just such powers.

"If, as far as we know, there are no other paintings by his hand, the explanation may be that he was soon to depart this life before he had time to paint any more."

The old aesthete fell silent. The lecture was over.

I invited the conservator home that evening. The August warmth enveloped the town, but a breeze from the west allayed the heat and made it comfortable enough to sit outside on the balcony in the dark. I served wine from Singing Valley; it wasn't new to my guest. He had long ago passed the social divide.

We drank the wine in silence and looked out into the night. The incessant roar of traffic rose from the street below. My wife joined us. We were all thinking about the painting, and how it could have escaped the attentions of the world through all those many centuries.

The size and subject-matter of the picture left no doubt that it had been painted as an altarpiece.

The solution was so obvious. It came of its own accord as I was raising the bottle to pour the wine. The label on the bottle showed a little village church in the mountains with the words *Church in the Valley* printed in a curve beneath.

"He can't ever have seen it," I exclaimed. "It's evident that the artist who designed this label had never seen the church in Singing Valley. But it doesn't matter, because no one else has seen it either. Nobody other than the people who live in the valley."

"So no one knew either that there had been a masterpiece hanging above the altar in the church for hundreds of years." It was the conservator who drew the logical conclusion.

"No, not until a bishop arrived in 1808 and robbed the church and the village of its sole treasure," my wife remarked drily, and took a drink.

"That sounds quite feasible, but it just poses a new question, which isn't so easy to solve," I said. "We don't know how this picture originally ended up as an altarpiece in a little church in an inaccessible valley. A painting that could have taken its place in any of the cathedrals of Europe."

There was silence again. We had no answer.

When my wife and I went on holiday later in August, we changed our original destination. We found ourselves walking along a track, or rather a path, that seemed to us totally perilous, following behind a horse led by an elderly man. We had slept out in sleeping bags for two nights. On both occasions we had made our camp on a flat spot on the mountainside from which vertical cliffs fell away abruptly on one side and rose up on the other.

We arrived in Singing Valley on the third day, just as the sun was setting. But before night fell we had caught our first sight of the little village. It consisted of about fifty small dwellings, built of stone, without mortar. Everything appeared grey and poverty-stricken. Even the people, of whom we saw nothing till the next day. They were all dressed in black.

The church stood on the edge of the cluster of houses. My assumption had been right, it looked nothing at all like the church depicted on the wine label. Obviously it was different from the other buildings, so there could be no doubt that it was indeed the village church we could see. But had it been transposed into more civilised surroundings, it certainly wouldn't have been so easy to recognise. Although the flimsy cross on the gable was a clear indicator.

Our guide over the mountains had promised to find us a bed for the nights we were to stay in the valley. Just as we were about to open the door of the church in our eager curiosity, he suddenly reappeared and asked us to follow him.

We went with him through the village. There wasn't a single person to be seen outside, but we could feel eyes watching us through the small windows of the houses.

The man stopped at a dwelling that was no different from

any of the others. I counted quietly to myself how many houses it was from the church, so that we could find our way back there again.

We were received by an old lady, in a friendly but unsmiling fashion. She gave us her only room, while she herself went to sleep at her neighbour's house. Before she left she prepared a simple evening meal for us. Dry bread and wine.

With a shrewd presentiment I lifted my mug and drank. Of course, the wine was the same as that drunk by the upper echelons of the Vatican on special occasions. It was younger, and obviously immature, but nevertheless had the characteristic taste that made the tongue tingle.

Before we could ask our landlady any questions she was gone; we just caught a glimpse of her in the half-light on her way to the neighbour's house.

The bed was far from cramped, it must in its time have accommodated a husband and children too.

But it was hard, with an underlay of straw. The night felt cold in the valley, and the little window apertures had no glass. The thin blankets that covered us didn't provide enough warmth. We soon got dressed again and climbed into our sleeping bags. Then we slept soundly until the next morning when we woke to find that the woman had returned.

She was making up a fire in the open hearth. Breakfast was identical to the meal the previous evening, dry bread and wine.

I remember that I was taken aback on that occasion twenty years earlier when I was offered red wine in the middle of the morning at my audience with the old Cardinal. Here in Singing Valley I soon realised that red wine for breakfast is perfectly natural.

It wasn't easy to question the woman. She answered monosyllabically. Only later did we discover, in conversation with others, that the dialect up there is very strange and difficult to understand.

27

It was the village priest who saved us from a totally wasted journey to the forgotten valley. He had come there after the death of his predecessor, and he reckoned on remaining there until his own death. He may perhaps have regretted his fate, but he didn't give expression to such a thought in words.

We went to the church again straight after breakfast. The door was ill-fitting and squeaked on its hinges when we opened it. The interior was small; the low benches had no backs. We turned our eyes to the altar. There was the altar-piece, an ordinary flat representation of Jesus on the cross.

Then the priest appeared by our side. He had entered silently by a door to the right of the altar. The door led to the priest's room, the place where he spent his life. He invited us in and cleared a space for us on the bed. He himself sat on a low stool. A box served as a table.

He was a young man. His hair was thick and cut quite short, with no sign of grey. His face had a glow of youthful determination. His cassock was made of coarse cloth that was in keeping with the impoverished surroundings. There was nevertheless something demonstrably proud in his bearing. He knew his calling and intended to fulfil it.

For the second time that day we were served wine in mugs, and it was barely ten o'clock. Again it was the same wine.

"I actually have the wine to thank that I don't starve," said the priest, "the way many of my predecessors certainly did. Since the valley became a supplier of wine to the Vatican, a tiny proportion of the revenue comes to the village church. It's enough for food and wine and the bare necessities of maintenance for the church. If I had to depend on donations from the congregation, it would mean abject poverty. There aren't many living up here now, and they're not great believers. They turned their backs on the church two hundred years ago."

"In 1808," said my wife.

The priest looked at her in astonishment, and nodded.

28

"Yes, in 1808. That was the year the priest up here made his big mistake, so big that I think God still regards it as an unabsolved sin. Legend asserts that the people here in the valley had received a wondrous gift from God, a painting depicting Mary and Child. And the legend goes that they acquired their ability to sing at the same time. Their voices rang out in the vineyards and in the houses. But they sounded best of all when they gathered in the church to give thanks and praise to God.

"Their voices were said to have filled the valley with their heavenly magnificence and to have shown that in their isolated existence they were at one with God and He with them.

"Thus they sang for centuries, up till 1808.

"That year a new priest came to the village. According to the legend, he represented evil itself.

"Personally I don't believe that, but coming to the forgotten little congregation in the valley seemed to him a punishment. The thought of spending the rest of his life here among these people was unbearable to him. I think it was that that caused him to falter.

"Three things really surprised him: the altarpiece, the singing and the wine.

"He himself had been brought up in a wine-growing region and had learned to appreciate a good wine. He was delighted with it, as well as with the altarpiece and the singing, but not as gifts of God that he could enjoy for all the years to come.

"No, the story goes that he immediately began to speculate on how these benefits could be transformed into quick profit for himself. In brief, he wondered whether with their aid he could speed up his own transfer back to a more populous area.

"Fairly soon after his arrival the priest sent a messenger with a letter to his superior, the Bishop of La Spezia. The people up here are in no doubt about the content of his message. According to them he described what he called the three wonders of the valley: the wine, the altarpiece and the singing.

"He must have been a good letter-writer. The Bishop's curiosity was aroused, not to mention his thirst. He announced that he would undertake a visitation to Singing Valley; it was to be the first and last in the history of the little church.

"It must have been a strange sight as the Bishop's retinue stumbled and struggled along the narrow path. The Bishop in particular had difficulties, his body was heavy and corpulent after many years of good living.

"But if he had regrets during the journey, his ill-humour vanished on arrival. The story is still told today of the Bishop's meeting with the village. Those who recount the tale don't see its comical side, they describe the whole thing with loathing. The parish priest met the revered guest as he rode into the valley with his companions and halted before the church. Though "rode" was hardly an appropriate term: the Bishop was clinging desperately to the horse's mane to prevent himself from falling off.

"The priest was carrying a pitcher of wine in one hand, a mug in the other. Even before the Bishop had dismounted, the priest had filled the mug and held it up to his eminent superior.

"The Bishop took the mug ungraciously and put it to his lips.

"He cheered up instantly. The wine was good. Was it just because he was so thirsty? He put the mug to his lips again and drank. No, it was still the same taste, an absolutely delicious wine.

"Now the local people of the valley crowded around the Bishop and his host. Immediately, the hills reverberated to the magnificence of their voices. The music was so beautiful that the Bishop was moved to tears, assisted by the wine with which his cup was constantly replenished.

"He then demanded to be shown the altarpiece that he had heard about. The story says that he tripped over the high threshold into the wretched little stone church and landed on all fours, though mostly on his belly, on the earth floor of the church. He raised his head in fury as he lay there.

"But he calmed down at once. Right in front of him, up above the altar, he saw the most beautiful altarpiece he had ever seen. And the Bishop was a connoisseur of art.

"The next day the Bishop busied himself with preparations for his return to civilisation. I think that his decision had been made the day before, at the very moment he saw the altarpiece. The painting could not remain here in this isolated valley. He must rescue it for civilisation.

"Or rather, he must have realised immediately that he wanted to send the painting to the Vatican as a gift, together with a few skins of the wine from the valley. He hoped it might persuade the Pope to select him when in the near future he had to appoint a new Cardinal.

"Anyway, according to the story, the intoxicated Bishop demanded writing materials on the table that very afternoon, and with great difficulty composed the donation letter that was to accompany the painting and the wine to Rome.

"The parish priest for his part approved the plan entirely: he had dreams of his own about the effects of the gift on the Vatican.

"The village church was full when the Bishop and the congregation celebrated a Mass for the return journey. The melodious song rose again. They all turned their faces up to heaven and praised the Lord. No one expected what happened next. After intoning the final prayer and blessing the congregation, the Bishop turned again to the altar.

"He advanced towards the painting whose home had been in their church since time immemorial and lifted it down. The legend states that everything went completely still; even the birds in the valley had stopped singing when the Bishop paused momentarily and cleared his throat.

"With an embarrassed expression on his bloated, arrogant face he told the congregation that he was going to take the picture to Rome himself. That was where it belonged, perhaps even in the church that Pope Nicholas had built many years ago on top of Peter's grave.

"Not with so much as a flicker did the villagers betray their feelings, but by that very omission they revealed everything. They uttered not a word of farewell, and the Bishop left the valley in resounding silence.

"At Vespers later that day the people of the valley gathered again in the church. It came as a shock both for them and the priest to find that, after centuries of miraculous singing, their God-given ability had disappeared along with the marvel itself, the painting of the Madonna and Child.

"Neither ever came back.

"The Bishop acquired his scarlet robe, and he was later remembered for the wine he brought to the Vatican. It still arrives every year in skins from Singing Valley."

"What happened to the parish priest?" asked my wife.
"He reaped no advantage. He was forgotten by the world beyond the valley and frozen out by his own parishioners. That is to say, he was starved out, dependent as he was on the gifts of the congregation. Unbelievably enough, it was over two years before he ceased to appear outside the church.

"Ten years passed before his superiors suspected something was wrong and sent a new priest to the valley. Only then was the skeleton of the evil and impatient priest taken out of the room at the side of the church and laid to rest in a grave.

"It was after that that a tax was imposed on the sale of the wine to the Vatican, as a punishment for the congregation. But also as a surety to keep the priest alive. The tax goes to maintain the parish priest."

Some of the pieces had fallen into place. An uneasy feeling came over us. We were sitting in the very room where the remains of the Judas of the valley had lain untouched for a decade. It was as if the priest had guessed our thoughts.

"I have to live here," he said. "All of us who have been priests here since 3rd May 1808 are atoning for an inordinate sin. A gift of God and a marvel were stolen from the people. My calling, and that of future priests here, is that of eternal penance."

I told him then of the painting's fate in Rome, of its hanging for almost two hundred years in the darkness of a sealed-up passageway, bringing joy to no one. He raised his mug sadly and took a drink.

There was no more for us to do in Singing Valley. The very next day found us again walking behind the man and the horse. We went very slowly past the dangerous places.

I could see the fat Bishop before me, he too on his return journey. How easy it would have been for the villagers to bring his expedition to an end here. They could have taken the marvel back in triumph.

But not unscathed in the sight of God, nor beyond the reach of the punitive arm of authority.

On the journey home we were lost in thought. That was when the car broke down. It was old and worn out. We were back in our own everyday life again, as if by a snap of the fingers.

We finally got to Rome by bus, tired and dejected.

We were dependent on the car; that is, my wife was. I promised her that I would arrange a loan straight away to buy a new one.

I went to the bank the next morning, introduced myself and explained what I wanted. To my surprise, after only a short wait I was shown in to the bank manager himself. I didn't think a routine loan for a car was such an important matter.

He was very friendly and arranged all the formalities for me to collect the money at the bank counter.

When I had signed the agreement and stood up to go, he grasped my hand and shook it warmly.

33

"Give my best wishes to your wife," he said. "I met her at a reception recently, she's extremely beautiful."

I passed on the greetings to my wife. She didn't remember him.

We bought a brand-new Alfa Romeo. It was she who wanted a fast car. I had to admit that driving it was a wonderful feeling. Nevertheless, I felt uncomfortable at putting ourselves in debt. My wife didn't.

I soon forgot the car. I was more preoccupied with the painting. It had created a sensation in art circles. Almost every day there were experts giving their views to newspapers. The first articles about the work were published in journals, and invitations were issued to seminars both in the Vatican and at the University of Rome in which specialists from all over the world took part.

I myself kept in the background. At the beginning I was interviewed by a few of the newspapers, as the man behind the discovery of the painting. But they soon found out that a librarian who has spent his entire life hidden in a manuscripts archive is not particularly interesting.

I could have become a centre of attention if I had told the story that the parish priest had vouchsafed to us. But I didn't. Nor did it emerge from any other source; either no journalists had visited the valley, or the priest hadn't told the story to anyone other than my wife and me.

Gradually the television and newspapers and magazines dried up, until a daily paper gave things a new twist.

Where should the painting go? What do our readers think? The response was enormous. Hundreds of museums and churches, known and unknown, were proposed.

No one, of course, suggested the little stone church in Singing Valley.

So I sat down and wrote a letter to the Council of Bishops.

I gave an account of everything I knew about the altarpiece and the marvels in Singing Valley.

My conclusion was unequivocal. I asked that the painting be returned to the valley and placed above the altar in the little church. That would right a wrong, not just against the inhabitants of the valley, but also against God.

The answer eventually came. They thanked me for my interest in the matter, but hoped I would understand that the proposal was unacceptable. They pointed out that the altarpiece had remained unknown for centuries while it had been in Singing Valley; if it were sent back there now, it would again sink into oblivion.

The painting is a masterpiece that belongs to the whole world, they stressed, not just to the inhabitants of one isolated valley.

They made no mention at all of the fact that the picture had been hanging for almost two hundred years in the Vatican Palace without being seen.

But in a separate paragraph they appealed to me not to pass on further the legend of how the valley had got its name. Romantic tales like that could so easily have an unfortunate influence on people in their search for God.

I discovered it early one morning: I could sing. Throughout all the years of life in the children's home I had been exhorted to keep quiet. I ruined every choir. I've always dreamed of being able to sing, but whenever I try, it's like the fairy tale: frogs come leaping out of my mouth.

I only made further attempts when I was totally alone, in the shower. And that morning: I could sing! Not like most people can; no, I could hear myself singing with a deep, magnificent voice. The unfamiliar Latin words rose up, it sounded as if the walls and ceiling of the bathroom were receding and expanding into an enormous cathedral. The ancient hymn swelled higher and higher into the vaulted space.

I didn't tell anyone of this fantastic discovery in the weeks that followed, not even my wife. And I was very careful not to sing in the bath when she could hear me. I was worried that she and others might believe that I'd lost my senses. Perhaps I had?

Anyway I was not in the least astonished when that same morning I found the package of old manuscripts in the archive. I knew what it contained the moment I stood with it in my hands.

The manuscript collections of the Vatican are enormous. Conservative estimates suggest 130,000 manuscripts and incunabula. Many of them are religious in nature, but almost as many are secular.

In my modest section alone there are eight permanent employees sorting and cataloguing the material, as well as all the researchers who engross themselves in it every day. But the material is overwhelming. At the rate we're going now, the work will never be completed.

So it's not infrequent that in this ocean of documents we find valuable old manuscripts that have long lain forgotten.

It happens much more often than with paintings, at least. Looking for a particular item in the welter of unresearched material is undoubtedly comparable to searching for a needle in a haystack.

But when I picked up a bundle of documents just before lunch time, weighed it in my hands and knew that it would tell me something about the painting, I was not surprised in the slightest. Not for one moment did I believe in coincidences. My new singing ability had cured me of that.

It is strictly forbidden to take manuscripts out of the archives building in the Palace. Despite that I smuggled the little package home with me. For the first time in twenty years

I broke the library's strictest rule. I couldn't wait till the next day to read them.

My wife was going out with someone for the evening. She was fetched by a car that hooted down on the street shortly before eight. I'd already been sitting for some while under the bright lamp at my desk. I hardly had time to look up as she kissed me and disappeared out of the door.

I had unwrapped the documents very carefully earlier that evening. The wrapping paper was indisputably of more recent date than the manuscripts themselves. They were very brittle and had to be handled with the utmost care, something I'm quite used to after all these years.

At about half past ten the telephone rang. A man's voice asked for my wife. He didn't give his name, but I was almost sure that it was the bank manager.

The papers were written in Latin, a language I'm not unfamiliar with.

Progress was very slow.

Nevertheless I soon found confirmation of what I'd surmised: the manuscripts I'd discovered were closely related to the painting.

When my wife came in at about three o'clock I was still sitting under the lamp. I didn't tell her about the telephone call.

The Writing on the Wall

They painted over the graffiti today. Two council workers appeared first thing this morning with buckets of whitewash and big brushes. They've been calmly and unhurriedly painting yard after yard of the wall all day long. It's gleaming at me now, pure and innocent in the afternoon sun. It's shining so white that it hurts to look at it. I miss the violent colours and the pithy comments with their black humour.

The prison warder consoles me: "They do that twice a year," he says. "Spring and autumn. They only paint it over to inspire the poets to new efforts. Just wait, it'll be messed up again in a week."

It happened as I feared it would. Once again the documents were deleted from the 'order list'. But I still get the wine, even though the Cardinal is dead. His successor obviously knows all about everything and is carrying on where the old man left off.

The Church is keeping a hold on me in another way too. My Father Confessor of many years ago has turned up again. He visits me once a week; the warder admits him to the cell at six o'clock every Tuesday. He presumably comes for my confession, but he never pushes himself on me. He sits down cautiously on the only chair in the cell, and I sit on the bed.

We talk a little about the weather. Then there's silence. I can see that he dislikes the situation as much as I do. Nevertheless he keeps coming back, Tuesday after Tuesday.

The priest is very old and he heaves deep sighs of resignation from time to time. I can remember him from the days when he was a young and enthusiastic head of the children's home. He was the one who took me in when I arrived there, seven years old and without a friend or relation in the world. He was nice enough, but I didn't like him. I didn't want to like anyone, or become attached to anyone.

I never spoke, neither to him nor to anyone else, about the terrible few minutes when I saw my mother die. Not until I met my wife.

There's nothing wrong with the priest, except that he lacks imagination. I still remember the Bible lessons of my childhood as unending and unbearable. He used to read the Bible the way others read a physics book.

Every week before he leaves he asks for us to pray together. The habits of the children's home are still there, and I clasp my hands and dutifully bow my head. He mumbles out a prayer whose words I can hardly hear. As soon as he's finished he gets up and says goodbye. He looks relieved every time.

Actually, he makes me nervous now that I've started writing. But neither he nor any of the others are going to stop me. I shall write down the truth.

THE FORGOTTEN PAPERS IN THE VATICAN LIBRARY

Vatican Library
Document MCLXXVII
Origin Unknown

The Painting

The artist left today. I would so much have liked to talk to him one last time, but he has gone. It's no more than a month since he arrived in this town on the Adriatic Sea.

I came here myself ten years ago; I felt at ease here. But everything has changed in the course of the last month.

When I realised that he'd gone, I went to the church, and I saw the picture for the first time. Now I know: the artist had the power to perform miracles. One look at the painting is enough to confirm that.

And he was right – by painting a background of evil he highlighted the purity in the woman. He should have known, the leader of the Council of Elders, that he himself has been portrayed in the picture, that his evil is there together with all the others' in the colours of the background and in the shimmering light effect. Perhaps that is exactly what he suspects.

I feel too that I have regained my faith. The marvel shining forth from the painting has also made an impact on me.

Something remarkable happened as I gazed at it and saw those shimmering specks of colour. How was it possible to create such an illusion of evil?

I stared, mesmerised, at the points of colour in the painting. They took on grotesque shapes before my very eyes. I couldn't relate them to anything I'd seen before, and yet they looked astonishingly familiar: they were hideous, distorted feelings from my own inner self.

And the shapes came to life, they merged and separated, turning into a seething mass.

No, they became a procession of people, a swarm of miserable wretches moving towards the top of a cliff and pouring over the edge like boiling lava.

Fire and brimstone was the image that went through my mind, and I shuddered.

I stood shaking and trembling in front of the picture. My eyes would not release their hold, they were transfixed.

Then the picture changed its character again, its evil slowly loosening its grip. The surface of the painting turned into cloth. The specks of colour were still there, soaking into the cloth and spreading steadily over it. The material, damp and red, folded itself over the picture and hid it from view.

I lost consciousness.

When I came round I was lying on the floor of the church in front of the painting, bent double with my knees pressed up to my chest. I looked up cautiously. It was Mary shining out at me once more.

I lay there for a long time before the painting in prayer.

I made my way slowly to the inn. All my strength had ebbed away, but I was filled with peace. I had taken the first difficult step on the path home.

By studying the painting of the Virgin Mary and Child I have finally come to understand what has been a mystery to me all my life: the eternally indissoluble bond between good and evil.

It's best that the picture shouldn't remain in the church where it was painted. It would be impossible. Like all other art it can only be ultimately redeemed when it is released from the history of its own origin. That can't happen here in this little town of shopkeepers by the sea.

But in another place the picture will be able to hang in peace until the day comes when it is recognised as a masterpiece.

*

44

When I found myself with the artist's notes in my hands, I thought at first that it must be a coincidence. But of course that can't be the case. On the contrary, I am the only one in the town who can say that I knew him. Not closely enough to call him a friend, but I got to know a great deal about him from his own lips. Things that a friend seldom hears.

In the company of a friend, a person is often silent about the thoughts that occupy him most, afraid of already having spoken them.

He must have been a good listener. His notes contain his version of stories he heard me tell in the marketplace on the five days he was going through his crisis. He came every day, except for the one he was ill, and sat in the circle of people around me.

The stories are not at all badly re-told. What surprises me is the seriousness with which he attended to me. So seriously that he must have misunderstood one or two things. When I now put these versions beside my own account of the artist I have to admit that I've altered a few phrases. I too have an artist's pride.

It has aroused strange feelings in me to see my own words written down by another.

Everything seems so different. Was that how it happened? By reading my words in his notes I saw so much in a new light.

For me too the time has come to leave. I am a stranger here. For the first time in ten years the idea of going back home has entered my mind.

His notes came into my hands this morning. I went to his house to ask after him, since he hadn't come to the inn last night. We had recently been in the habit of meeting one another there as dusk fell. I missed him as I sat there drinking my wine. My friends beckoned me, but I stayed sitting on my own in the hope that he might eventually arrive.

A woman opened the door and shook her head when I asked for him this morning.

"No, he's gone away," she replied curtly. Her negative response sounded rather like a defence of the absent man.

In an attempt to learn more I told her that I was an acquaintance of his, and that he hadn't turned up to meet me at the inn as we'd agreed. I noticed that I had avoided using the word "friend". It might have been this honesty in the description of our relationship that inspired her trust in me.

"Wait a minute," was all she said, and disappeared. A moment later she returned with a package in her hands.

"This is the only thing he's left behind. He won't be coming back. You can take it."

I wondered why she wanted to give his papers to a chance visitor. Now that I've read them, I realise that she must have been carefully instructed on whom she should give the package to.

I took it hesitantly. I was on the point of handing it back again, but my inquisitiveness prevailed. I had a presentiment that it contained the answers to my questions.

That was how his notes came into my possession.

I am the storyteller here in this town. I've had that role for almost a decade. I arrived here after fleeing from myself. When I came riding down from the mountains one day to this town on the east coast, my thoughts were to find a bed for the night, as was my wont; a few hours' sleep and then on, always onwards.

But that evening was different; something told me to stop. As I sat in the semi-darkness of the inn after satisfying my hunger, exhaustion crept over me. Not just the usual tiredness after a day on horseback, but an apathetic torpor that spread through my body and mind. The warm red wine from the jug in front of me had an immediate effect, and I felt my restless unease disappearing, like a liberation. For the first time in months my despair receded, and left me in a pleasant state of indifference.

I asked for another jug of wine and can remember the woman's smile as she put it on the table. But I can scarcely remember her and her husband shaking me awake and helping me to my room.

I slept for almost twenty-four hours. The sun had already set when I woke again. I spent a second evening in the cosy parlour of the inn, drinking wine and absorbing my new feeling of peace. And once more I went to bed and slept. The next morning I went for a walk round the town.

Before I returned, I had sold my horse to a man in the marketplace. That was when I realised I had decided to stay. I still had enough money for a few months' board and lodging at the inn. Time would determine what I would do next.

The innkeeper and his wife were fine, good-natured people, full of laughter and concern, and also sensitive enough to leave a person alone with his silence. It came intermittently, when occasionally my defences were lowered and the past flooded in. Eventually I would learn how to protect myself from it, by constructing a shell to keep out my earlier life.

Only in sleep did I still remain defenceless.

I enjoyed my life at the inn. There were regular customers who came every evening. At first I sat outside the closed circle of people, but I felt almost as if I were taking part in their conversations.

After just a few evenings I was brought into their company. Their curiosity was friendly, but never intrusive. I soon began to feel I was one of them. And over the wine in the semi-darkness I began telling stories.

I've always been keen on telling stories. I have a good memory and I learned a special technique from an elderly storyteller in my youth. It helps me to commit tales to memory and to recall them again.

The men round the table thought highly of my stories and encouraged me every evening to tell more. They listened with pensive expressions as I spoke. From time to time they would raise their glasses to their lips, and often put them down again without drinking. I was encouraged by their attention, and continued to bring forth a stream of anecdotes.

One evening, some months later, one of my new friends came to the inn and told us that the town's old storyteller had died. He had told stories from his permanent spot in the marketplace every day for forty years. My friend thought that I ought to take over from him. The others agreed.

I sat and thought over the proposal for a while. I wanted to, but would I be capable of it? Did I have a large enough stock of tales and legends, and even more importantly, had I good enough sources for new ones?

The others had their answer ready: as a lodger at the inn I had the best chance of hearing new material. It's frequented by travellers who visit distant places and bring stories back with them. Fairy tales and romances have always followed the paths of the caravans.

You have to like people to be a storyteller, like them and be inquisitive about them. I won't deny that my interest in the artist who had gone away also included an element of a possible new tale.

I decided to try. The next day I went to the marketplace and took up position in the vacated spot. I cleared my throat nervously to attract attention. That was how I started as the town storyteller.

I never met my father, and he never saw me. He deserted my mother and his home before I was born. But history repeats itself – he also stood in the marketplace every day and addressed the public. He didn't tell stories as I did, he forecast the weather. He was a weatherman, and enjoyed great respect in his profession for a long time. I feel a great urge to perform when a crowd assembles around me in the marketplace, and I must have inherited that from my father.

For the first few days there were lots of people gathered on all sides to listen. That's how it always is when you're new.

Gradually they became fewer. I went in daily fear that everyone would lose interest and that there would just be empty space in front of me. There's hardly a better hint that it's time to make way for somebody else.

But the sign didn't come; after a while the decrease in listeners came to a halt. From then on the numbers remained steady and slowly climbed again, year by year. Today I have my regular audience who I know enjoy it and whom I myself feel happy with.

There are always some newcomers too, often travellers who stop to hear the storyteller without knowing of him in advance. Quite a few of them over the years have sought me out in the evening at the inn to oblige with a tale that they themselves have brought. That's how I increase my collection as time goes by.

Fortunately, what people like most of all is to hear again something they've heard before. The joy of recognition is instilled in us all from childhood. You can also be saved by someone in the audience asking for a particular tale, thus assuming responsibility for it on behalf of the others. It's the most rewarding for the storyteller too, since a person who has made such a request always feels he has to throw in an extra coin.

The good storyteller is seldom short of material. Recounting a story about someone is different from experiencing it in reality. If you live through something as it occurs, you're always restricted because you're ignorant of the thoughts of the participants.

A storyteller doesn't worry about such things. He pretends he's inside the minds of his characters, and thus knows all their thoughts. He chooses an ending he asserts to be the right one. That's how he creates tension in the story. The next time he might select a different mind and a different ending, which he proclaims as the only true one. On a third occasion he will create the tension by not getting into the mind of any of the characters at all.

In reality I am an incorrigible fabricator who always chooses the explanation that suits me best at that moment. Nevertheless I always think that my endings are probably closer to the truth than what was generally imagined at the time. Because people and the lives they lead are quite complicated.

So, I earn my bread by telling stories, which doesn't make me rich, but neither do I starve. To tell the truth, I have amassed a considerable amount of money in the years I've stayed here. My personal needs have never been very demanding. I've enjoyed a simple life at the inn for ten years, where cheap wine has been my only self-indulgence.

These savings will be of use now. I shall go to the leader of the Elders and ask if I can buy the painting. I'm fairly sure they'll be glad to rid themselves of it. They associate it with nothing but unpleasantness, and they can't perceive how beautiful it is.

I always had sufficient money in my previous life. In that existence there was one mind I never managed to find my way into, and that was my mother's. She concealed her innermost thoughts from everyone. She never uttered a word about my father. What little I know, I've heard from others. That, of course, was from those who wanted to share their knowledge with me. Over the course of time I've put it all together to give what I think must be a true picture of him.

I grew up in a large house with lots of servants. My mother was rich and very lonely. She died suddenly when I was still a young man. I inherited everything.

The artist – I won't mention his name, because I never used it in my conversations with him, nor did he use mine – came to the town at the instigation of the Elders. He was a painter much in demand even though his features were still youthful.

He had served his apprenticeship as quite a young boy with one of the great masters of the time in Florence. Now he was travelling on commission from town to town painting altar-pieces in churches.

I followed the discussions that preceded his assignment here. There are many who now, with hindsight, disclaim all responsibility. And those who originally proposed the idea are investing a lot of energy in explaining away their error.

But a good number of the foremost men of the town are just keeping quiet, putting up a palpable wall of silence around themselves in these difficult days, as there often is around people who are tormented by their conscience.

Naturally enough it's the town Elders who bear all the responsibility for what occurred, that little group of power-brokers who pull the strings when they want something to happen.

In reality they are a self-appointed Council who have complete control over everything that takes place in the town. The appellation "Elders" does not reflect the whole truth: it's not enough to be old to belong. It's money that counts. Only those who rule others by means of their personal fortune can take up a position on the Council.

It consists of ten members, sufficiently few to create a permanent battle for places. But ultimately it's one man who decides who will have a seat. He is the self-elected leader of the Council.

He is also the local moneylender, and has for years advanced loans to the most disparate people and on the most unusual terms. He thus holds the entire town in an iron grip and is the man with the real power. A place among the Elders has its price, and it is the moneylender who cashes in on it.

It was the Elders who brought the idea of a new altarpiece to the town. Many of them travel regularly to other places on business. Those who travel have experiences, even if not everything is suitable for recounting on return. But they did speak of the new art in other churches.

They discussed the matter among themselves in the Council. Most of them considered that a new picture, painted specially as an altarpiece for the church here, would bring them honour. Even the moneylender was of that opinion. It was therefore a happy coincidence when news arrived from the neighbouring town that raised envy among the inhabitants. It too is situated by the sea and has developed as a trading centre in the course of the last century. Over the years great rivalry has grown up between the two.

Because of this the news was received very gravely on the day it became known that the neighbouring church had acquired an altarpiece, a pictorial representation of the Holy Madonna and Child. Travellers spoke of a beautiful painting that had a remarkable power. Never had so many sought the house of God in that town before. It was said that worshippers in the pews felt closer to the Lord since the painting was put in place above the altar.

The power of envy is strong. The marketplace was in turmoil for the first few days after the news reached town. Nor did the agitation die down. People kept angrily asking the same question over and over again:

"Why haven't we got a painting like that in our church, to the glory of God and for the enjoyment of all of us who live here?"

It was thus natural for the matter to be raised by the Elders at their next meeting. In fact they had really decided the question long before. They announced that the town would be adorning its church with a painting of the Virgin and Child.

There was much rejoicing when the decision was made known. The people flocked spontaneously to the house of the Lord in the middle of the day and gave thanks in prayer and song.

Who would paint the picture? They had no artist good enough to carry out such a task, they all realised that. But, as everyone knows, there are many competent artists nowadays who travel around from place to place.

The desire for a pictorial representation of the divine is not a local phenomenon, even if there are individuals here in this town who maintain that they thought of the idea first.

After lengthy consideration the final choice was for the same artist who painted the picture for their neighbours. He was a respected painter, but not too well known. That made the price acceptable to the Elders.

Someone also had an idea of where he could be reached, and their emissaries had no difficulty in finding him in the next town, the one on the other side of the mountains, where he was in the middle of working on yet another altarpiece.

The negotiations were straightforward, their representatives had had precise instructions on how high they could go with their offers, and the moneylender had assessed the situation with his usual skill. They thus quickly came to an agreement with the artist on both price and general conditions.

The latter included board and lodging for the duration of the work. The artist reserved to himself the free choice of potential models for the Madonna and the Child, and the finished painting would be accepted when the artist himself regarded it as complete.

The envoys returned home satisfied, and were received with jubilation.

So was the artist when he arrived two months later with his little entourage. They were followed in triumph to the house that had been prepared for them in the meantime. Admittedly people had assumed he would come alone to take up his commission in the town, but they nevertheless respectfully welcomed the woman and child who accompanied him.

"No," he replied in answer to questions, it was not his own family but the models he had chosen for the picture he was to paint.

A special room had been designated in the house for him to paint in, but he immediately made it clear that there could be no question of working there. He wanted to create his painting on the spot, in the church. Only by doing that could he take account of the light in the area where it would hang and thus create a picture in which composition and setting and light would be as one.

The empty room was furnished for the woman and child instead.

Nobody had any objections to his wish to paint in the church, as long as he didn't work on holy days. This solution had a significant additional advantage: in the church everyone could come and go all through the day. And there they could also follow the creation of the painting from the first moment to the last.

At the outset the artist didn't seem disturbed by spectators while he worked. If they kept still and didn't talk he was happy to let them watch from a distance as he started painting.

In the first few days only one or two people slipped inquisitively into the church to take a look. There wasn't much to see, and they didn't stay long.

The board on which the picture was to be painted comprised three pieces. It was mounted on an easel set on the floor. The first week was spent preparing the surface. The artist brushed several coats of glue on it, and filled the cracks with a mixture of glue and sawdust. The whole process took time: the board had to dry thoroughly between each new coat. He used a knife to scrape away any unevenness to produce a smooth but not too shiny surface.

When the sizing of the board was finished he tore up strips of bleached linen that had been boiled in advance to remove any trace of grease. He dipped them in glue and spread them over the picture surface. He smoothed them out with his hands to remove all unevenness in the joins. Then he left the board to stand and dry again.

I can describe this in such detail not because I was there watching him at work, but because he told me about his methods afterwards, over a pitcher of wine at the inn.

During these lengthy preparations the artist also attended to the positioning of the woman and child for the painting. They were both with him in the church from the very first day. He made a careful study of the light shining in through a high window in a concentrated shaft down towards the altar. The light had to fall on the woman's face in a very particular way. He corrected her position again and again, rearranged the folds in her simple dress and showed her how to hold the child. He also made charcoal sketches on paper, experimenting until he was satisfied.

At the beginning, those who visited the church were disappointed. All they saw was the artist preparing the board before he could begin painting. But, for lack of anything else to speculate about, they became increasingly interested in the two people there, the artist and the woman.

Everyone who saw them was touched by the tenderness and patience he showed in his guidance. Some of those who visited the church insinuated later that they had noticed the man's attraction to the woman even then: that his instruction went beyond the professionalism of the artist.

Possibly they were right, even if the artist himself in his naive innocence didn't realise it. What everyone else could see had not yet impinged on his consciousness.

His affectionate intimacy and concern brought out a reflection in her eyes that gave a perfect illusion of the Holy Mother. Her face was filled with an infinite purity and peace that permeated the whole church.

His confidence gave her the strength to believe in her own role as the one chosen by God. That's what those who saw it said.

In the ensuing days, it was the woman's face that was the subject of conversation in the marketplace. All who had seen it tried to convey their impressions, the feeling that it really was a Madonna sitting in the church.

At that stage there was a constant stream of people coming to the inn every evening gossiping about the woman and the artist in the church. I didn't understand their excitement, and had no plans to be among the spectators myself.

Then suddenly everyone wanted to go there to have a look at the woman. The numbers increased so much that eventually a huge animated crowd of people were all trying to push their way into the church at the same time. As might be expected, the artist's patience was exhausted and he packed up his painting equipment in a rage. The woman wrapped her cloak around her face, and together they returned to their house. He locked himself in and remained there for two days, until the Elders sent him a letter expressing regret for the disturbances.

It was decided that the church would be closed every day while the artist was working. I later came to realise how delighted the Council were to be able to do that.

The very next day after this decision he was back at work, along with the woman and the little child.

Now people gathered instead on the streets when the two of them were on their way to or from the church. Everyone wanted to catch a glimpse of the woman's face, both those who had seen her before the closure, and those who had simply heard about her beauty. But nobody's wish was granted, because her face was covered for her hurried journey along the streets with the artist.

Nevertheless, or perhaps precisely because of that, the gossip about her didn't cease. In the marketplace, and everywhere else that people congregated, she was constantly being described.

Thus expectations of the painting rose, they were formed and nourished by the closed door of the church and the veiled face of the woman.

The church was open to people as usual on Sundays, and they poured in. They were disappointed to see that the easel holding the painting had been moved to one corner and covered with a cloth. Three chalk crosses on the floor marked the place where it stood when the artist was working.

No one could complain about his diligence. He went to the church with the woman and child at the very break of day. They didn't return to their lodgings until sunset.

A woman was employed to keep house for them. It was she whom I met on the occasion when I looked for the artist at home. She went to the marketplace daily to buy food. She cooked for them and served them a meal in the morning before they went to the church, and in the evening when they came back again.

In the marketplace everyone wanted to talk to the housekeeper. Could she say anything about the artist and his woman? Was she as beautiful as people made out?

There wasn't much she could or would say: they did very little in their lodgings, apart from eating and sleeping. And yes, she was beautiful.

The housekeeper wasn't one for gossip, she felt it was part of her job to protect these people she had been appointed to look after.

But there was also another question in the minds of many, even if they didn't dare put it into words: did the man and the woman share a bed?

The housekeeper held her tongue about everything that happened within their four walls, but her very silence was interpreted in such a way as to arouse further curiosity.

Despite all this, I was inclined to take the general inquisitiveness at that time as an expression of anticipation. Everyone was looking forward to the moment when the consecration of the Madonna painting would take place.

The Elders, on the other hand, were constantly convened in endless meetings. From the day the painter and the woman arrived here in the town, an inexplicable anxiety had taken root among them. Nothing was discussed openly, and no announcements were made from the Council meetings. More and more people realised that something was amiss.

Finally the Council took a decision, though not one that cleared the air. They would pay a visit to the church to have a look at the work that was now in progress.

The artist didn't like it at all, but he didn't refuse them admission. He went on working sullenly, while the Elders gazed at the painting and at the woman, but mostly at the woman.

He told me about this strange visit when I met him for the first time that same evening at the inn. He was sitting there with a glass of wine and a gloomy face when I walked in. I was immediately inquisitive, I admit, and asked if I might join him. He nodded mutely and not very invitingly. He wasn't easy to communicate with at the beginning. But he gradually thawed, helped in good measure by the wine. Then he showed both his artistic temperament and his youthful, naive ability to have faith.

Instead of reproducing our disjointed conversations of many late evenings, I will rather let him speak through the papers he left behind. I understand him better now that I've read his notes.

4th March

When I rode down towards the town this afternoon, I felt a flood of conflicting emotions. It's beautiful here. As I came over the hill and saw the terracotta red of the town against the blue sea, it was the colours that made an impression on me. I raised my eyes to the mountains and saw the evening shadows already gliding up from the valleys to the peaks. My weariness, which has been so burdensome lately, vanished at once. The ridges of the mountains were turning purple, the stars seemed close.

It felt like a release, a confirmation of the miracle I experienced two days ago. I know that I can paint again, and that my strength is returning. Things have been difficult lately; my last picture was never completed. It lacked God's liberating blessing.

When I entered the town itself, my feeling of peace left me. I was met by people shouting and laughing; they frighten me. What are they rejoicing for? Me? The picture I'm going to paint for them? I suspect something dangerous in their easily aroused emotions that could take an unexpected turn. Perhaps it won't be as easy to rediscover my creative ability as I thought up there in the mountains.

But at the same time it feels good to have the woman with me; she makes me feel secure. She shall remain a stranger to me, but I have a peculiar feeling, both definite and yet obscure at the same time: that she will give me the strength again to paint the pure features of the Madonna, the chosen woman loved by God.

I was certain immediately I saw her among the throng in the streets. Her face distinguished itself from the crowd, it was beautiful and had a purity in the eyes which for one brief instant reminded me of a feeling of deep sorrow.

She wasn't angry when I stopped her, nor even surprised.

I felt embarrassed when I said who I was and what my intention was. That I *must* paint her, that she would be the ideal model for a portrait of the Madonna as an altarpiece in a church.

"Not just a model," I quickly added. "When I look at you, you are a Madonna."

That caused her some astonishment, perhaps because of my halting speech. At the same time it looked as if her eyes lit up from within, where a moment before I had seen sorrow.

I had to continue on my way: I was travelling to another town the next day to paint a picture in the church there. Would she, in all decency of course, accompany me there and sit for me while I painted? I put the question, even though I felt I knew in advance that the answer would be negative.

So at first I didn't believe it when, after a short pause, she raised her head and said yes. There was no one and nothing to keep her in the town. But she would have to bring her little child with her.

I looked at her and realised that she meant it. It must have been God who had seen my distress and heard my prayer. He had sent me this woman, a living Madonna, to set free the artist in me. Her little child was just a confirmation of the miracle, the Mother and Child.

The next morning I arrived early at the agreed meeting place. Would she come? I had hardly closed my eyes all night. I could see her constantly before me.

Even before the appointed hour I saw her in the street with a little child on one arm and a bundle in her free hand.

I took hold of the infant carefully and laid him in the basket that was strapped to the side of the mule. Equally carefully I helped the woman up into the saddle. We rode out of the town together towards our new destination.

5th March

I haven't begun to work seriously. I walked around today to view the town. It forms a natural harbour by the sea. The colours that made such a strong impression on me when I was riding down from the heights are even more beautiful at close range. There are flowers growing everywhere already in bloom. People tell me that this region is called the Floral Coast.

6th March

I have had my first working day in the church. I've set up the easel and the folding board. It has to be prepared, but I save a lot of time when I don't have to begin entirely from scratch. Placing the woman was almost a matter of course, where the light falls in a concentrated beam from the high window. She is the ideal model, willingly following all my instructions.

On my walk through the town yesterday I cut some twigs from the willow trees growing down by the beach. Back at the house I chopped them into pieces as long as the span of four fingers. Then I bound them tightly together and buried them in the warm ashes of the fireplace. When I dug out the bundle again in the morning they weren't burnt up, but turned to charcoal. I was lucky. If the sticks lie there too long, they easily smoulder and burn. If they are there for too short a time, it's impossible to draw with them. These were perfect. When I drew with them on the paper, the charcoal dust formed a thin layer. If one line goes wrong, it doesn't matter. Because when I've finished, I score the right strokes with a silver point. That binds the charcoal to the paper. Then I blow the loose charcoal away, and the clean drawing remains.

I've made many sketches of the woman today, varying the position of the easel and board. I've drawn her from all sides. Now I'm sitting with the sheets of paper in front of me, trying to choose the best angle. What is constant is the dignity in her bearing, reproduced in my lines.

At the beginning of the day the church was almost empty. Then gradually a few people arrived. They watched us as if we were odd, exotic creatures. I hope they soon grow tired of that.

7th March

Previously I've never minded people watching me while I work. It's different now. It's as if they're not spectators any more, but active participants in an evil game. I can no longer see the woman's face without it being at the same time hunted and devoured by the many-headed pack behind me.

8th March

I cannot bear people's prying eyes on the back of my neck any longer. They're coming to the church in increasing numbers to satisfy their curiosity. It was really bad today, it seemed as if the whole population of the town was trying to enter simultaneously. It was impossible to find any peace to work. I could see in the woman's face that she found it as unpleasant as I did. They just stand there staring at her.

My work on the painting is of no interest to them while I'm still preparing it.

I became furious. I turned to them in a rage and screamed out my anger. Then I packed up my things and we went home. We won't go there again until they close the church.

10th March

They have closed the church to spectators. It was a new experience to come back and be able to hear the silence. Even the light falls differently in an empty church.

A curious thought. My picture will be different in the empty space from what it would be like in a full church. Different and more original.

I have begun painting. It was easy to sketch out the figure on the board; I know it in my fingers from the sketches I've prepared.

15th March

It's wonderful to sense my joy in work returning, along with my creativity. I am painting again. My old master should have seen me now. He would have liked my brush strokes, they're sensitive, there's body in them, and I'm executing them with a confidence that feels as if my hand is being steered by God.

It's strange to feel Him so near. I've never done so before, I've never even been sure of His existence. Now I know that without it everything is pointless. A painting without God's pledge would be just an empty surface.

I shall not paint a picture that explains; faith cannot be explained. It disappears in the light of reason. No, my work will be a prophecy of the incomprehensible, of hidden reality.

Only thus can miracles be painted, by grace. As a mystery.

My teacher, whom I think of as the old master, did not believe in God. I remember how he used to snort when anyone called on a higher power.

"A painter is driven by his own strength," he would thunder. "If you don't have that, you're no painter and no God can help you."

I feel strong. Today I know that I'm a painter, and I believe that God is helping me. It's good to be able to write that.

It's been a depressing time since I realised that I could no longer paint a picture of the Holy Madonna without faith of my own.

Now I have emerged from my melancholy as a new person.

As a sign He has sent me the omen of the woman and child. With her in the light by the altar I can create again. In her I can read God's promise to me.

When I say this to her, I can also read the affirmation in her eyes before she mutely lowers her gaze. I can see that it makes her happy, even if she doesn't say so.

She hardly ever talks to me; she is silent every day for all the hours we are in the church except when she is murmuring to the child who is sitting on her lap or toddling with cautious steps around her. She herself sits solemnly and patiently. She has the patience of an angel, and puts every effort into following my instructions. Even if it's painful to hold the same position so long at one stretch, she never gives up. She has taken a burden upon herself and is determined to bear it.

Only when I take a break myself can I get her to move. Then I hear her low voice for a few minutes as she sings to the child or talks and plays with him while they walk about in the church.

As soon as I give a sign of recommencing work, she takes up her position on the chair again; she knows exactly how it should be and is very conscientious about getting it right.

I have started grinding and blending colours in a different way from before. It must be the light out here by the sea that gives me new abilities. I've managed to retain the clarity of the colours while at the same time giving them a special surface when they dry. It adds a delicate tone to the painting that enhances its elevated subject-matter.

But for the Madonna's face I use the old method that my master taught me. First two brush strokes with a mixture of green ochre and white lead in a tempera of glue and egg. Then I mix the flesh colours, for which I have to take care to use eggs from a town hen. The yolks are lighter than those from country hens and are thus more suitable for the skin of a young person.

I'm quite obsessed by the Virgin Mary. I've painted her for many years, again and again; despite all my efforts I still don't know her.

I shall never know her, that's what I have to understand.

Even so, she has come so much closer to me during these last few days. She is with me in the church as I paint.

I constantly think of my teacher, Cennino Cennini. I worked for him for fifteen years. He taught me all I know about painting. He in turn had learned his craft for twelve years with Agnolo Gaddi, who had worked for his father, Taddeo. And he had worked for twenty-four years with the greatest of them all, Giotto. A fine tradition has been placed in my hands. Only now for the first time do I know that I can take it forward. With God's help.

18th March

The Elders have announced that they will visit the church while I'm working. I don't want to deny them admission, but I can feel the anxiety rising in me again. What is it they want? Why can't they wait until the painting is finished?

These people are concealing something behind their impassive faces. When we meet any of the Elders on our way to or from the church, they turn away instead of greeting us. These are the same people who were so friendly when they were negotiating with me about the painting.

19th March

The Elders came today. They just gazed at Mary. I've started calling her that now, to myself. I'm uneasy. I don't want to have any more distractions now.

If there is anything they are displeased with, they should say so.

20th March

I went to the inn last night to calm my unease with a jug of wine. Fortunately there weren't many people there. An elderly man, the town storyteller, sat down at my table. I kept quiet at the beginning, wanting to know a bit more about him before entering into conversation.

The man can't really be described as old, even though his long hair and beard are almost white. Beneath a high forehead his eyes are still alive and inquisitive. His nose is straight and his mouth small. In the part of his face not covered with beard there are furrows bearing witness to the years he has lived. He is short and thickset, and dresses simply, in black. He still has the bearing of a proud man, but I can see that he likes his wine. He told me that the inn is his home. He's lived there for ten years.

He was friendly, and I decided to talk to him. I drank more than I should. So I also talked too much. He let me talk.

Of course I soon blurted out my anger about the Elders' visit to the church. It did me good to get it off my chest. He just gave a faint smile at my outburst, as if he knew more about the matter but didn't want to say so.

When I think about it afterwards, he said very little about himself. He hardly said a word about the time before he took up residence at the inn. And whenever I questioned him, he deftly turned the conversation back to me again. The only thing he said was that he came here as a fugitive.

It helped me to talk to someone. He's not the sort to carry gossip further.

It was Mary I talked about most, the earthly Mary, the one sitting in the shaft of light in front of the altar. I tried to explain the wondrous thing that's happened to me, God sending me a living Madonna to give me the strength to paint her as she was, chosen and blessed.

I talked about my work, too. About technique, how I prepare the board in the way I was taught. Through all the years I was with the master I was the one who did all the preparatory work, even for the boards he used himself. It is instilled in me how important preparations are, not only for painting, but also for achieving peace of mind.

It's obvious that the white-haired man has that peace of mind, even though he says he doesn't believe in God. In that, he's the same as my master.

I also spoke about how easy it is to have one's peace disturbed. About being pestered and bothered by all the inquisitive townsfolk, and about the anxiety caused by the Elders' incomprehensible visit.

He is the town storyteller. He has his fixed site in the marketplace where he goes at the same time each day, the fourth hour after the sun reaches its zenith. He sits himself down with his audience around him and tells his story.

I think he's a clever man. I'll go there myself one day and listen to his stories. I also want to go to the inn again this evening. I need someone to talk to.

I've made an important decision today. About the painting. I'm going to have a serene blue background for the Madonna. It must be the proximity of the sea. Every day I see the play of light between the sky and the sea in the hour after the sun has gone down, each in different shades of blue.

Up to now I've always used an ochre background in my paintings; that was what I learned as correct.

It has also become more usual recently to paint the Mother of God against a landscape background.

The perspective of landscape can create an exciting tension in the picture.

I think blue is better, it emphasises the purity.

I use Baghdad indigo, which I mix thoroughly in water, blending in a little white lead.

21st March

I didn't go to the inn yesterday. Mary is ill. After we got home yesterday evening she collapsed on her bed. It wasn't until I heard the child's persistent crying from her room that I realised something was wrong.

She hadn't complained once during the course of the day, though I'd noticed that she wasn't quite her usual self. She hasn't been ever since the Elders came on their tour of inspection.

I found her now fully dressed and unconscious on her bed. She was clasping the sobbing child tightly to her, without being able to do anything else for him.

I took care of Mary first. I loosened her clothes and bathed her feverish skin. It's the first time I've been near another person's skin since I was very small. Her body was as perfect as her face. I've seen naked women before – my teacher used models – but I've never touched a woman.

I tended her as carefully as I could and helped her settle into a good position for rest.

Then it was the turn of the child, and again I felt joy streaming through me as my hands touched him. Luckily he wasn't sick; his temperature was normal and I could feel his little heart beating.

As I laid the child at her side, I couldn't help absorbing her silent gratitude.

If it hadn't been so cool in the church, I would have asked for the child to lie naked in his mother's arms.

I must send a message to the woman who keeps house for us, so that she can look after Mary and the little one.

Madonna

If he had only told me all that, I could perhaps have helped him, prepared him for what was to come. Because I suspected that something was wrong, something quite dreadful. I knew the people of the town, and over the last few days I'd felt the growing unpleasantness in the atmosphere.

But I didn't know him. I'd drunk wine with him just one evening, we'd scratched each other's surface, but that was all. I guessed nothing of his new and still burgeoning faith, no more than he himself was aware of his own love.

He had unwittingly revealed that to me on the first evening. He kept constantly repeating her name, in an embarrassed, rather touching manner.

Though I'm not sure whether I would have acted any differently if I'd known more. What could have been done?

I didn't believe in a God myself, and hadn't done so since childhood.

I've never been very interested in the Virgin Mary. I've never before thought of the conception and birth as a miracle. Not until now, having seen the finished painting. I'll probably be in a state of confusion from now on.

Never before have I wanted to subject myself to the idea of one will and one omnipotent grace. Fundamentally I preferred the concept of several gods each watching over his own area. It provided a better answer to the games chance played with human beings. Especially if I imagined that some of them were just as malicious as humans themselves can be.

Besides – and this is the most difficult thing to change – I'd finished with everything that goes by the name of love between man and woman. It had caused me far too much pain, even in all the lonely years I've lived here. I didn't understand it. It wasn't as straightforward as I once thought, nor as absolute as I needed it to be.

Or, it is even simpler, and just has to be accepted, not understood. That has been my theory on the matter recently.

Now that I no longer reject God, it is he, the artist, who has turned everything upside down. My thoughts are dominated by him, and I know I am holding on to him with the grip of envy.

I wouldn't dare say that to anyone, let alone write it down. Still, now that I have turned to God again, it doesn't matter so much any more.

Could I have prepared him for what was to come? Should I already have told him the story of the servant girl at the inn, the tale I myself heard in the tavern only a short while ago?

I don't think I could have helped him. I only know that that was my fervent wish on the evening he next sat opposite me at the inn. When everything had already happened, on the 22nd March according to his own notes.

22nd March

They have been here, the representatives from the Elders. The leader of the Council, the moneylender, was himself among them. It was he who spoke and told me that the model I have brought to the town is a whore in her home town beyond the mountains.

They behaved politely, but they made it clear that the

Elders cannot allow the woman to sit any longer as a model in their church.

As if I would want it.

He came into the inn that evening and drank more wine than he could take. He was in despair, wanting to talk about it yet at the same time not wanting to.

He was a tall, rather thin figure, his face still young and vulnerable-looking. His strength was in his eyes. They were deep-set, beneath a smooth forehead, in a face which that evening was full of pain. It made a powerful impact on me when he started to weep. The tears ran profusely down his cheeks, and his shoulders were heaving.

He had been let down both by God and by man on the same day. So it seems that punishments can be co-ordinated. If indeed it was a punishment and not just one of life's chance events.

I let him weep and poured out more wine every time his glass was empty. What else could I do?

Should I have gone into the truth for him? Should I have told him that the Elders had obviously recognised the woman on the very day she arrived in the town? That they had put off revealing it not to spare the woman, but to hide their own shame?

Should I also have told him what he still didn't know: that he loved his Mary? The time was hardly right.

I filled up his glass.

As I did so I knew it was to absolve myself. I didn't want to get involved at all, not again, in matters to do with God and with love. I was afraid.

I know what I thought: only when the whole thing is over

and passions are dead will I be able to formulate my story of the painter and his Mary.

Only then can I add *my* contribution to it: detachment.

23rd March

I got drunk yesterday; how did I make my way to bed?

Now it's all come back to me – they were here yesterday and told me that my Mary, whom I called "my miracle", is a whore.

She whom I so firmly believed to be God's gift to *me*, conditional upon my fulfilling my pledge as an artist.

It is all just the vain, self-obsessed dream of an inadequate painter.

If there's anyone who has tricked me into seeing purity in her face, it's the devil.

I remember the words:

"A painter is driven by his own strength. If he does not have it, he is no painter, and no God can help him."

There is no God and no devil.

I am no painter.

Mary is a whore. I dare not go to the church and see the truth in the painting. A whore painted by a mediocre fraud.

I'll never go to the church again.

I met the storyteller at the tavern yesterday. Does he really have the right to call himself that? He had nothing to say or tell, he just mumbled and kept refilling my glass. What was the point of that?

24th March

Yesterday I could hardly get out of bed. I just lay there dozing. Everything that's happened came back to me in terrible visions. I didn't sleep, but had nightmares nevertheless, gruesome colour images that paralysed me.

They threw stones at the house tonight. All the windows facing the street are broken. I could hear the frenzied cries from the furious crowd outside. They're the same ones who cheered us when we arrived here. I didn't go out to them. Luckily our rooms are on the other side.

When it went quiet, I heard Mary weeping. What had she expected? I didn't go in to her.

Later the same day

Nor did I go to the church when dawn broke. I can't. But when the time came, I left the house and went to the marketplace. People I met in the street lowered their eyes and hurried past me. They are probably the ones who stoned our house last night.

I found him straight away, the man who calls himself a storyteller. He was sitting in his place with a group of listeners around him. I'm sure that he saw me, even though he gave no sign of it. I know that it was for me he told the story of a girl called Mary.

Another story about Mary.

A folk tale, he called it. Was it the story of *my* Mary?

I am confused and ashamed.

I saw him the moment he arrived in the marketplace that day. His face was white with despair. He sat down in the circle around me, but couldn't settle. He kept getting up and sitting down again.

I told him the tale I'd heard myself at the inn only a few months before. It was a merchant who'd told it. He'd come from the town on the other side of the mountain.

The artist looked so restless and shaken that I didn't think he'd understood it. But there I was wrong, he had written it down very carefully; I found the story among his papers. I have appended both this and the other stories I told him, in his versions. Only occasionally have I found it necessary to make corrections to them. I have also let his own comments stand.

A Folk Tale

This was the first story I listened to in the marketplace.

A young woman allowed a stranger into her bed because she thought he was an emissary of God. She became pregnant.

That was how the story was told as gossip in the marketplace, and at the beginning it caused mirth. How could a girl be so simple?

The storyteller stared out over the audience in front of him and a glint of anger came into his eyes.

I can see it, you're laughing too. That's a sure sign that you think yourselves superior to her. But I can tell you there's no cause to.

In the town where she lived, the laughter soon turned to scorn. And from scorn it was not far to indignation. Shouldn't she be chased out?

The girl had never had parents. She had been found one morning as a baby on the steps of an inn. The couple who owned the inn had kept her, but that didn't provide her with a family.

As soon as she had learned to walk, she had to work for them. She never received any praise, but was scolded and beaten when things went wrong. At night she slept in a little room in the loft. She rose early and went to bed late. She worked the whole day through.

When she was old enough she was sent to the marketplace

to buy food. Every day she carried meat, fish and fresh vegetables back to the inn. She enjoyed these daily expeditions: they were a release from her prison for a short while. But she never spent longer than necessary at the market, because she knew what would be awaiting her if she did.

Nevertheless it was in the marketplace that she met the boy who was to become her friend. He noticed her while she was conscientiously haggling over the price of vegetables. He liked what he saw and spoke to her. She's not too fine, he thought. She was shy and afraid to smile, but when she once did so he felt it as a caress. He accompanied her back towards the inn, but he was soon unable to go any further in case she was seen.

Some time passed before they met again. She came to the market every day, he went there seldom. But one day he turned up as a customer at the inn.

She approached the table hesitantly and welcomed him. He ordered his food and she brought it to him. More customers came and she was busy. The youth sat following her with his eyes as she ran between the tables. He liked what he saw. Eventually he got up, took his leave and departed.

But he came back. The very next day he was again sitting at a table in the inn. He soon became one of their regular customers. He came almost every day after he'd finished work. He was an apprentice and would soon be a journeyman.

When there weren't many customers, he and the girl exchanged a few words, but beyond that they never met one another.

It was therefore difficult for the innkeeper and his wife to understand when one day the girl told them that she and the young man wanted to get married. Not immediately, but when he'd completed his apprenticeship.

The girl could hardly comprehend it herself. Just once, when there were no other customers, they had held hands, and he had pulled her on to the bench beside him. She felt warm with joy when she stood up again. It was the first time she had felt a touch as a caress.

But it wasn't until a month later that he asked her if she would marry him. Swiftly and without drawing breath as she put the food on his table. Her answer was even more inaudible. A nod and a visible blush.

The landlord and his wife weren't very happy when the girl told them. She was good, cheap labour for them that they were reluctant to lose. On the other hand they didn't want to offend the young man either. There weren't that many regular customers and he now took most of his meals at the inn.

They decided to let time run its course. So much could happen, there was still a year to go before the youth completed his apprenticeship.

And indeed much did happen, and the landlord and his wife were quick to assist as soon as they saw a chance to frustrate the girl's marriage.

One evening there was a new customer at the inn. He was a stranger, a tall, commanding man. He had a full black beard streaked with grey, his hair was long and well-groomed, and he had a sharp, straight nose. But it was his eyes people noticed. They were dark, with an inner fire.

Everyone looked at him the moment he came in. His broad-brimmed hat with a feather was already in his hand. He wore his cloak with careless assurance, and unfastened it and hung it up while greeting the inn and all its customers with an imperious gesture of his hand.

The girl noticed him too and felt a peculiar disquiet. She wished her fiancé were there, but he had gone away for a while with his master, who was building a house in another town.

The stranger was a lively man. He immediately caught everyone's attention with his good humour and infectious laughter. Soon they were all listening to his discourse. As the evening progressed, a relaxed, friendly atmosphere developed.

The young girl became aware of it as she ran between the tables. People were nicer than they usually were. No one shouted abuse when they had to wait. No one pinched her when she leaned over tables to mop up wine from an over-turned glass. They smiled at her instead, and some even gave her a coin as thanks.

It's the stranger I have to thank, the girl thought. It was he who created this atmosphere.

She realised the man was following her with his gaze, and on one occasion their eyes met and he smiled at her. She blushed and bent her head. Again she felt uneasy within herself.

The evening came to an end, the customers drank up their wine and went happily out of the tavern. Finally there was only the stranger left. He called the landlord. Could he put up a guest for a night or two?

The landlord prevaricated and played hard to get. He thought all his rooms were occupied. A coin changed hands and he remembered the empty room up in the attic. The stranger thanked him, but asked if he could sit a little longer down in the tavern until he'd finished his wine.

"Gladly," said the landlord, "but my wife and I would like to go to bed."

He beckoned the girl over and asked her to stay, in case the guest wanted anything else.

He may have given the man a slight wink as he wished him goodnight and left the room.

Most of the lamps were out, there was just a single flame on the stranger's table. The gentle draught cast a flickering reflection on the whitewashed walls. For a while the man leaned silently over his table. The girl was sitting half asleep on a bench by the kitchen door.

Then he called her. Not in an impatient way, as she was

77

used to. His voice was friendly. She rose quickly and went over to his table.

Did he want more wine, she enquired. He shook his head, but at the same time invited her with a gesture of his hand to join him at the table. She perched hesitantly on the bench opposite him, and remained there uneasily, with her head bowed. She was tired, but at the same time oddly excited. It was quiet again for another few moments.

Then he began to talk, asking her about this and that. Did she like it at the inn? Was the work hard? She answered in a low voice and in monosyllables, but she soon recognised the warm, friendly atmosphere from earlier in the evening.

Nevertheless her trembling unease was still there. She could feel her body quivering.

When she looked up, she was captured by his dark eyes holding her fast in his gaze. She didn't know why, but she started telling him everything. About the hard toil at the inn, about beatings and thrashings. For the first time in her life she opened up to another person.

He heard her attentively, smiling and shaking his head. Never before had anyone let her open her heart, not even her betrothed.

It was as if the stranger could guess her thoughts: did she have a boyfriend? She blushed and nodded, and told him. That he was five years older than she was, and a craftsman. That he came to the inn every day to eat so that they could be together.

The customer listened to her, nodding attentively. Suddenly he raised his hand and placed it gently over hers on the table.

She jumped with fear and drew back her hand. He pretended not to notice, and let his simply stay there.

"It's late," she said, but immediately fell silent. It wasn't the servant girl's place to be the one to take her leave.

"Yes," he said, "but I have something to say to you."

He rose quickly to his feet and picked up the jug.

"Is the wine barrel in there?"

She leapt from the bench and tried to grab the jug. He pushed her gently but firmly down again. He lit a lamp and went out. When she came back, she had laid her head in her arms on the table. She hurriedly raised it.

He had brought an extra glass, half filled it and handed it to her. She took it, but set it down straight away. He filled his own and held it out, wanting to drink with her. She lifted her glass unwillingly and took a sip, but didn't like the taste and put it down again.

The stranger sat without speaking for a while, emptied his glass and refilled it. Then he shook his head and continued sitting in silence, but obviously thinking hard.

"Listen," he said, "I come with a message for you." He seemed unsure of himself for a second, but then went on. She could feel the solemn words rendering her incapable of action, and lowered her head.

"Look at me," he said in a commanding voice. She obeyed, and was trapped by that look that held her in thrall.

"I have been sent here by God; He has chosen you to bear Him a son. He shall be sacrificed for the sake of mankind. A virgin shall bring him into the world, and you have been found worthy. I am Gabriel, the emissary of God. I bring His seed to you."

He didn't let go of her eyes. She felt she was struggling, as if in a fever. Spasms passed through her body and she was overcome by a dull lethargy. When the stranger took her hands now, she didn't pull away. Nor when his hand stroked her hair and continued down over her shoulders and her back. She began quietly weeping.

Then he took hold of her and pulled her gently up. He embraced her.

She let it happen.

But when he held her away from himself again and went

to kiss her, she tore herself free and fell backwards. It was the acrid smell of sour wine that woke her.

But now Gabriel was patient with the girl no longer. He gripped her hard and shook her. She hung limply in his arms as he thundered:

"Submit yourself to the will of the Lord!"

The warmth and friendliness in his voice had vanished. He released her and she sank to the floor.

"Go to your bed," he said, "and keep yourself in readiness."

The girl rose as if in a trance. She staggered across the room towards the stairs.

"Do not bolt your door," the voice went on, as she slowly made her way up the stairs, clinging to the rail.

He poured himself out some more wine, and sat down to enjoy it. And he went out to fill the jug again.

Then he took the lamp and climbed unsupported up the stairs to the attic. She had locked her door, but it was old and ill-fitting and gave way at the first kick.

Gabriel stayed three days at the inn. Three nights he went to the girl's room. She no longer had the strength to resist and obediently received the seed he gave her in God's name.

It wasn't the girl who told of what had happened. She carried on with her work at the inn without a murmur.

But the landlord and his wife could not keep quiet. Gabriel had also vouchsafed to them his divine task. On the last two evenings he sat drinking with them for a long time before going to the attic to perform his duty.

They both took delight in spreading their version of the story. It reached the marketplace on the very same day the stranger left the town.

No one believed that the girl could be entirely guiltless in what had occurred. Hadn't she sat up half the night drinking wine with a stranger? The glasses on the table the next morning were evidence enough.

Thus the tale of the shameless girl became known, spiced as it was with the account of Gabriel and his divine seed. For that was included in the story – the young girl believed that the stranger was the messenger of God.

When it turned out that the girl was pregnant, the gossip increased. This time it also reached her betrothed in the neighbouring town.

He heard the story from a traveller in consternation and dismay. Setting out in a state of turmoil, he hastened back to his home town.

As soon as he stepped into the tavern and saw his beloved and the landlord and his wife, he knew that it was true: it was indeed to him that it had happened.

He stood for a moment as if paralysed, then turned and went. He was a carpenter, and she never saw him again.

The girl went about her work as the child grew within her. She moved heavily among the tables. She listened in silence to the mockery from the customers whose wine she poured.

When the time came, she lay alone in her room.

Down below in the tavern everyone knew what was happening, but no one went to her aid. No one was there when the birth took place.

At first, both mother and child went on living at the inn. She toiled as before. The landlord and his wife were thinking of the future: they would soon have two to work for them.

The woman was again sent to the market to buy food. Now she had the child with her. People wouldn't leave her in peace: as soon as she appeared, they heaped abuse upon her.

The innkeeper and his wife wrung their hands helplessly. Was it their fault that the girl had acted shamefully?

They soon turned to lamenting their lot. The girl was a young hussy who was bringing them into disrepute. The inn would get a bad reputation if they allowed her to carry on living there any longer with the child.

So they threw her out.

She stood on the street with the child in her arms. She had nowhere to go and no money for food. In desperation she began to trudge round the town in search of something to eat.

But no one is ever entirely alone, not even in a situation as hopeless as that. He soon turned up, the man who made his livelihood from women's misfortune.

Before sunset the young mother and her child had been found lodgings in a little room in a house he owned. She was still unclear about what the future held in store for her. But before the night was out she knew. And by the very next day it was common knowledge that the town had got a new whore.

"We might have known," said the innkeeper and his wife. "That's the sort of girl she was."

From then on she encountered only silence on the rare occasions when she hurried through the streets. That was how the good citizens wanted it.

24th March, continued

When the storyteller had finished the tale of the unfortunate woman, the circle of people around him was completely silent. He had spoken in a low voice, but quite clearly enough for nobody to have difficulty in hearing him.

I myself was confused, and could feel a flush of shame rising to my face. How quick I'd been to condemn the poor woman as soon as I knew she'd been a whore. Without any doubts about my own righteousness, I'd been ready to cast the first stone.

I was the one he'd told the story for, to make me understand. He didn't do it last night, when I was agitated and angry and also rather drunk. He had waited till today, till the time when the after-effects of the wine were still in my head and I felt dreadful.

I could feel remorse rising in me, together with despair.

What thoughts hadn't run through my mind? I'd sensed my fury surging up: the woman had to be punished. In my imagination I had whipped her. And I'd enjoyed it, I'd seen her cowering before me beneath the blows.

What sort of person am I?

We sat in silence round the storyteller, each lost in his own thoughts. Then I plucked up courage and asked, almost inaudibly:

"What did the young woman believe? Did she believe that it *was* actually Gabriel who came to her, sent by God?"

The storyteller looked at me almost as if he had been expecting that question. Nevertheless he pondered for a few moments before answering.

"I don't know," he said hesitantly, "but I've begun to think about something more important: if she believed so at the time it happened, what about today? Does she still believe she has been chosen by God? Does she do so despite the humiliation she has experienced?"

I sat there feeling a slender hope growing inside me.

But then a young man in the crowd opened his mouth. With a note of obstinacy in his voice he expressed his faith:

"I'm sure she does."

I felt a twinge of jealousy. What right had he to know anything about Mary?

That was *my* right, and I still had doubts.

Then the storyteller spoke again:

"Something else happened. In one way people's eyes were opened by what had occurred. They suddenly saw that the young woman was exceptionally beautiful. But that didn't help her in her misfortune. Beautiful whores are just more in demand."

In the background someone laughed.

On the way home from the marketplace I decided to talk to her.

But I am still hesitating as I sit here thinking over the situation. I haven't talked to her since the truth about her became known. She's been lying sick in her room all this time, and I haven't visited her.

I must tell her about the order from the Elders, that her former life has been revealed and that she can no longer model for the Holy Madonna.

I wanted to tell her that I don't blame her for anything, but that she has to leave the town.

My first impulse when I found out the truth had been to throw her out. In a black rage I wanted to strike the woman who had hurt me so deeply.

It's my self-respect as an artist that she has destroyed. Blinded by her external beauty, I had built up a false belief on which to base my vision. She was the instrument that gave me the right to paint the pure Mother of God.

For one fleeting moment I had found in that belief the confirmation of myself as an artist.

My anger has evaporated now. I understand, and also recognise that she grasped the opportunity to escape from her fate. I forgive her.

But I cannot forget that she has annihilated me as an artist. I can only ask her to take her child and leave the house.

So he too suffered from hubris; I hadn't realised it till now. But wasn't it to demonstrate this to him that I had told the story of the weatherman the following day? No, I had begun to come to terms with my own hubris, my inheritance. Without a thought for the young, naive artist, I had started to seek my own inner self.

Nevertheless he listened to the story and felt himself accused. Innocent young man. For him there is still hope.

Hubris

This was the second story I listened to in the marketplace.

A man was overwhelmed by desire. He confused it with love. Since he wasn't able to control either, he tried instead to control the weather. He fared badly, because the weather too follows its own inscrutable laws, unperturbed by mankind.

The man was a weather-forecaster, and had stood in the marketplace every day for many years declaiming his predictions. He was an expert. He had served a long apprenticeship with his father, who in turn had learned the art from his father.

The father had taught his son to be observant of natural phenomena and heed their signs. That was how he gradually discovered connections that could be used to predict the weather. The frog croaks before rain, the swallow flies high when good weather is coming. There are many such portents, and the young man learned them all. Through new observations he also found other indicators to assist him.

On the day his father retired, the son appeared in the marketplace and forecast the weather at the top of his voice. He made a good start. Week after week his predictions were fulfilled. He was proud to note that his reputation was growing, and as luck was with him, he also inherited the respect the townsfolk had had for his father.

He was successful, and the people liked him.

Time passed. No one could compete with him, and his right to a fixed place on the square was never in doubt. Only on one occasion did a tradesman try to erect his stall in the weather-forecaster's corner. He also proposed, with shameless impudence, that the daily forecast should be written on a board and hung on his stall. It would be practical, he thought, because people wouldn't have to turn up at a particular time of the day to hear the weather report. They could read it any time they had business in the market.

The trader was chased out of town. The people wanted to hear the weatherman's voice. He carried on with his announcements.

But no one can survive such adulation in the long term. It probably wouldn't have been so bad if he hadn't enjoyed the attention so much, but the admiring gaze of the crowd made him rather supercilious. He started thanking God for making him so much more competent than any of the others.

He didn't lose his accuracy; that wasn't the problem. What he gradually lost through less detail, he made up for in greater skill. He was still very competent.

But he developed bad habits. His voice took on an affected sound, he no longer read the forecast, he intoned it in an artificial and exaggeratedly ponderous manner. In that way he was able to extend his performance and enjoy the admiration of the crowd for a greater length of time.

He also developed his own affected way of walking. And when he raised his arm to get attention, it was with a pretentious gesture that became more noticeable every year. There were some who found him a comical figure, but among the hordes of his admirers they kept their views to themselves.

But that was not the case with the young girl who stood at the front of the audience one day. She burst out laughing at the sight of this middle-aged, puffed-up man.

Thus did misfortune strike. The weatherman heard the infectious laughter and quickly discovered where it was coming from. Before him stood the most beautiful creature he had ever seen. He was older than the girl's father, but suddenly as much in love as he should have been in his youth.

He had to stop halfway through his predictions, temporarily overcome; in staring at her he had lost his concentration and didn't regain it until everyone had noticed what had happened. Only by calling on all his reserves of strength did he manage to re-focus his mind and complete his forecast.

The girl disappeared into the crowd, but her mocking laughter haunted him long after. He couldn't forget her, and every day he prayed for God's help to find her again. But it was no good: she was gone.

He should have let it rest at that. Instead he committed the most foolish act of his life. He consulted the Elders to ask for their assistance. He blushingly admitted that he wished to find himself a wife. They were full of sympathy and ready to come to his aid. One of them immediately expressed a willingness to offer his own daughter: the thought of acquiring the weather-forecaster as a son-in-law was not unwelcome.

Several of them had unmarried daughters, and all of them were anxious to help.

Still feverishly excited and somewhat incoherent, the weatherman struggled to explain that his eye had already fallen upon a particular young girl. He didn't know her name, but described her as he'd seen her standing before him in the marketplace.

The Elders exchanged meaningful glances, but were still willing to assist. The girl could and should be found – and indeed, in a few days she was.

They called the girl's father and told him the glad news. He went proudly home and conveyed it to his daughter. She was far from happy. She wept night and day, to no avail. But since she was a practical girl, she eventually realised that she could hardly withstand the will of so many men. With apparent compliance, she accepted her fate.

But in her heart she swore revenge, not just on the weatherman, but on the whole town.

When the wedding took place, she was a calm and dignified bride. In an unwavering voice she gave her consent to the blushing man. There were some who even then suspected that in her the weatherman had got more than he'd bargained for. Putting on his arrogant expression, but still flushed, he gave thanks for his bride with as much passion as he employed to trumpet out the weather.

Until that day he had lived a modest life. His house was small and rather dilapidated. He had cooked his own meals, and once a week a woman had cleaned the two little rooms. Things would have to change. Even before he was allowed to touch his beautiful wife she had made him promise her a more elegant home. The infatuated husband complied with her wishes straight away. He would look round for a new house the very next day.

The weatherman scarcely knew what he was saying. All he could think of was the girl's body. After the promise was made he was allowed to take ecstatic possession of her. He slept happily, freed from his torment.

The next morning she had already been up for a long while when he woke. He felt desire rising in him again and called for her.

But this time he didn't have his way with her. He had to get dressed obediently and eat the meal that was on the table for him.

Then he was reminded of the promise of the previous night, and before the sun went down he had bought a large and magnificent new dwelling.

She wanted it redesigned. The work was completed before they moved in.

Their married life soon took on a regular pattern. She would only agree to go to bed with him after he had promised to carry out her wishes. There was always something new. And so the house filled up with possessions. Servants were engaged, and horses appeared in the stable to draw the new carriage.

Again and again the husband gave in and complied with her demands. He had no time for discussion. The day had already been far too long for his desire.

Thus passed the first year of their marriage. She never let him take her body for granted. If he wanted to possess it even for a moment, she had a counter-demand ready.

The weatherman was caught in a trap. Like a trained dog he now carried out his wife's slightest whim almost before she had expressed it. So she found it quite easy when she asked him for a room for herself in the new house.

"I would like to have somewhere to go with my girl-friends in the mornings," she said.

Her husband was blinded by love and harboured no suspicions. He got workmen to fit out a room next to the bedroom. Furniture was procured according to his wife's desires, and he was delighted by her enthusiasm.

His joy soon came to an abrupt end. On the evening of the day the room was finished, she withdrew into it and locked the door behind her. The lovesick husband stood outside it in stupefaction. In a whisper, afraid that the servants would discover his pitiful situation, he tried to persuade her to open it.

Eventually he burst into tears and besought her to come out. She was unyielding, and in the end he had to slink back to the bedroom to spend the night there alone.

The next morning he was met by a good-tempered wife who mentioned not a word about the wretched events of the preceding night. All day long he fussed around her, trying to ingratiate himself.

"Is there anything I can do for you?" he asked. "Just say."

There was. When night came and they were about to go to bed again, she said she was willing to share his bed if he would grant her one wish.

"Just name it," he said with relief.

"It's not a difficult one to fulfil," she said. "Tomorrow in the marketplace I want you to forecast rain and storms."

The weatherman's composure was quickly shattered. He stared at her. Did she mean it? Did she want to make him a laughing-stock?

"My profession is probably the oldest one of all," he said. "It's given by God to the chosen few. It's His knowledge that I bring to humankind. I could never mock Him or myself in such a way."

She gave him no more than a shrug of her shoulders as she prepared to withdraw to her own room.

"And besides, there won't be a change in the weather now," he went on. "This is the most reliable period in the year. There'll be sunshine for weeks to come."

"As you wish," she replied. "Then I'll bid you goodnight."

Once again he held her back while he feverishly sought a way out. But there was only one open to him. He gave in; the thought of another solitary night filled him with despair.

He heard himself in astonishment promising his wife he would do it: he would go to the marketplace the next day and forecast storms.

When morning came he almost forgot to go off as he'd agreed. But eventually, with dragging steps, he went to meet the calamity that awaited him. All the signs pointed to continuing clear skies and hot sun. There was great consternation when he pronounced his warning to the people, particularly perhaps because his voice did not have its usual self-important sonority.

Was he serious? He could hear the murmuring increase to a fully-fledged hubbub before he was out of the marketplace. He crept home in humiliation and went to bed in the middle of the day. For the first time he did not seek out his wife when evening came.

That night there was a violent storm. The rain beat down

and the wind raged. The weatherman stared out into the darkness at the miracle. Beside himself with joy he rushed out naked into the tempest, and stood in the black of night feeling the rain against his skin. He was filled with relief and rapture.

When he realised his honour was saved, he was overcome with a feeling of humble gratitude: he dropped to his knees and gave thanks to God.

Back in the house, he embraced his wife in gratitude to her, too.

But his humility soon disappeared.

When day dawned, all the Elders came as a group to pay tribute to him and bring gifts. Other prominent townsfolk also came streaming in with presents and speeches of praise.

His walk to the marketplace that day was a triumphal procession. The streets were full of people, despite the storm. They shouted to him in jubilation and followed him along the way. When he reached his corner of the marketplace, it was full to capacity.

The leader of the Elders stepped forward again; he was of the opinion that in future the weatherman should be called the weather-maker.

The crowd joyfully added their refrain, crying in unison: "Weather-maker! Weather-maker!" as they followed him home.

His wife was waiting. She too dutifully called him "Weather-maker", as everyone else was doing.

That night God revealed Himself to the weather-maker in a dream.

"You are my favourite among men," He said. "I shall send my predictions through you. Your wife is the unknowing instrument."

Life once again resumed its normal course. He performed his task with even greater solemnity, and quickly became accustomed to his new title and dignity. He was filled increasingly with an intoxicating sense of power, eliminating all doubt.

He basked in the reflection of his own brilliance and took pleasure in his lovely wife. But in one sphere everything remained as before: she would never let herself be taken before he had agreed to her latest wish.

That was how she had kept his desire alive. Only things that are freely available become a habit. He was also now so rich that it was never difficult to accede to any demand. Gifts came flowing in from people he knew and from those he didn't. Life smiled on him and he was happy.

But he had stuck his head in the sand and refused to see where things were leading. He was therefore quite unprepared when one day she again wanted to involve herself in his weather forecasts.

He refused even more determinedly than the first time. He slept alone for three whole nights before he gave in and asked her to expound her prediction.

For a moment he was relieved when she said she didn't want to interfere with his daily reports. But then came the shock: she was thinking of the outlook for the next week, a long-term forecast. He protested: it wasn't possible to verify predictions of that nature.

He was utterly terrified when he heard her announce in his name:

"God will send a flood upon the earth. From the third day of next week the rain will pour down night and day for ninety days. Only those who listen to the weather-maker and follow his advice will be saved."

He slept alone for one more night. Then he gave up his resistance. The possibility of yet another miraculous prediction was gradually occurring to him.

At midday he announced the long-range forecast in the marketplace.

This time the reaction was frightening. People surged towards the weather-maker's corner in panic, crying for help.

He remembered his wife's words and repeated them to the crowd:

"Gather your possessions together and make for the heights." Again it was his wife's words he was using.

But now the sounds of the words mingled with a sense of power within himself. As before, he felt a connection with God, and remembered that his wife was just His instrument. He was conscious of his strength rising, and in a forceful voice he cried out the words that were welling up inside him:

"Fear not, for I am with you. I will lead you to safety myself."

A mighty cheer greeted him. Never was his power greater than at that moment.

On the morning of the second day of that week he assembled his servants and told them to take everything of value to safety. But his wife stopped him.

"Let us not think of ourselves in this fateful hour," she said. "We'll leave our possessions here."

When he looked at her doubtfully, she quickly added:

"Go to the marketplace and carry out your heavy responsibilities. Lead the people to safety. I'll get myself ready and join you."

A restless crowd was waiting in the marketplace. They lacked a leader. He felt a sense of his own importance as he formulated his orders. The people heeded him in blind obedience and followed his slightest instruction. Very soon his selected assistants were reporting that everyone was ready to go.

A strange procession set off. They were all bearing their belongings on their shoulders, and those with small children were angry that they had to leave their valuables behind.

There were few elderly men and women on the expedition: most of them were abandoned to their fate in the town.

"That's how it has to be," they said, and consoled themselves with the fact that all the others were in the same position. The old were written off as lost in a natural disaster that had already taken place.

The column could be seen for hours from the town, weaving its way up the side of the mountain like a sinuous snake. Those who watched it were the elderly and infirm and a few who didn't believe in the weather-maker's prophecy. Among the latter was the weather-maker's pregnant wife.

Before night fell, the snake had disappeared from view. The people had reached the plateau at the top of the mountain. They gathered in groups, tended their sore feet and made fires.

The weather-maker was very busy going from group to group, offering encouragement and advice. He gave orders for all food to be collected in – it had to last for ninety days and would have to be shared out in small quantities. Now it turned out that many had just brought valuables and left their food behind.

For a short while he also searched for his wife. He assumed she was hiding from him and became rather angry. Why hadn't he knocked her fancies out of her right from the start? It was going to be different, he promised himself, once the flood was over. Then the thought occurred to him with a shudder: imagine if it didn't come!

He shook off the fear immediately and continued his rounds. He calmed and consoled. They looked upon him as a prophet.

After everyone had lain down to sleep, he himself prayed to God. He prayed fervently for a flood upon the town and its people. They really deserved it. Then he too settled down to sleep, but he didn't close his eyes all night.

At sunrise the sky was just as blue and clear as before. It

94

gave no cause for doubt. A God who punishes chooses His own time.

But after another night, when the sun rose on the second day and there was a mild, pleasant breeze in the clear air, unrest began to spread. It increased during the day and towards evening it was only a few sensible citizens who prevented a crowd of youths from stoning the weather-maker.

After the third night on the mountain top, at sunrise he was nowhere to be found. He had begun his descent from the mountain under cover of the receding darkness. They could still see him far below, and now nobody could prevent the angriest ones from throwing stones. They didn't hit him. He got down unscathed. He didn't return to the town, and no one has seen him since.

They would have liked to have met him, all the people who crept down from the mountain during the course of the day and slunk into the town.

For the next few days hardly any men went to the marketplace; only the women went, because they had to, to buy food. But soon everything was its old self again. Life went on, and people's thoughts once more became arrogant and full of hubris.

25th March

The storyteller has seen right through me. My own hubris was so obvious. I was the only one who didn't see it.

I was willing to forgive *her*! With what right do I hand out forgiveness?

I am the one who should beg for it. I have offended God with my arrogance. It was my hubris that made me feel insulted as an artist. My vanity is repugnant to me now.

I need forgiveness from both God and Mary.

*

Fortunately I didn't talk to her yesterday as I'd intended. I would have asked her to leave the house. Now we can leave the town together. I don't want to force upon the Elders a painting they don't want. I shall complete it somewhere else, far enough away for Mary to be freed from her unhappy past. I shall take care of her and the child.

Everything must change.

27th March

But events have taken a different course. This time the misfortune is irredeemable, and it's my fault. As I sat writing, I was suddenly overcome by fever.

In no condition to visit her, I collapsed on my bed and was no longer aware of the world around me. I lay like that for almost a day and a night, the noises from my surroundings just reaching me as disparate fragments. It was dark in the room, and I was only conscious for short periods at a time.

I wasn't aware of the woman until the next day. She was washing me with gentle hands, and stroking my forehead tenderly. When I was able to focus my eyes again, it was Mary I saw, and I felt strange sensations flow through my weakened body.

For some time she hid her face from me, but when I eventually gazed into it, I could see that she knew everything. The sorrow I had suspected the first time I saw her was openly visible now. Again I was struck by her beauty, by the purity that radiated from her like a halo.

For one moment the thought passed through my mind that that is what she looks like, the Holy Madonna. And suddenly I heard the storyteller's voice again:

"Does she still think she is chosen by God?"

Now I knew the answer. She had believed it because God had let *me* tell her. From the minute I stopped her in the street and told her, she had believed.

When I looked into her eyes now, I could see that her conviction had gone, replaced by an infinite sorrow. Because I had failed her.

Everything must change, I thought.
Then I fell back into a deep sleep.

It was the middle of the night when she came to me. She lay down with me, and when I embraced her naked body I knew that that was what I had longed for ever since I saw her for the first time.

The anger that had taken hold of me disappeared. Her body was near, and its warmth and tenderness spread rapidly to mine.

Cleansed of my spent fury, I lay there feeling her caresses bring out a yearning desire in me. A desire to be touched, to be intimate, to stroke her ardent skin tenderly, to be close to another human being and feel the blood and warmth flowing through her. To find a mutual harmony and melt together as one.

I was in love; for the first time I knew what the word meant. She was pure in her affection. All feelings of shame and all my previous thoughts had vanished. I love Mary.

Today I awoke rested and refreshed. I could feel that my strength had returned, and my power as an artist.

Mary was no longer with me in the bed, but I knew she wasn't far away.

When I went into her room, she wasn't there. The child and the few possessions she had brought were also gone.

She has left the house.

She has left me at the very moment that I have found her.

In my blind egotistical need to worship myself I have destroyed everything.

Through hubris. The storyteller was right.

I noticed the change in him as soon as he arrived that evening.

He'd been through both heaven and hell since I'd last seen him in the marketplace.

By that time I had become his confidant; he needed someone to unburden himself to. The woman he had brought with him had gone. After he had finally understood his own feelings, she had disappeared. She must have left the town, because he had searched for her everywhere. He had roamed around all day since early morning in the desperate hope of finding her again.

I told him that it was probably best that way. After the truth about the whore became known, a storm of indignation had raged through the town. It was directed at the woman they had worshipped, who had deceived them all. If they found her now, she would have been in danger.

Hardly anyone blamed the painter, he was one of them, deceived, fooled like everybody else into thinking that the beautiful woman was a worthy model for the Holy Madonna.

Nor was there anyone who had a bad word to say about the Elders, even if they, in exposing the woman, had undoubtedly revealed their own wretched shame.

That evening too it was the wine that helped the young artist. At the beginning he kept wanting to go out and continue the search. Then he calmed down for a while. For the first time in his life he had found love and had given free rein to his emotions. Again and again he spoke about Mary and his longing for her. And repeatedly broke down in despair. What must she be thinking of him?

She must obviously believe that he still regarded her as a whore, and that that was how he had thought of her when she came to him in the night.

I assured him it wasn't like that, that she knew his feelings. Indeed, that she had known of his desire long before he had admitted it to himself, and that she had come to him so unreservedly precisely because she knew.

But he didn't believe me.

I had to use different words. When I went to the marketplace the next day, it was to tell a story about the inner essence of love, a story of how miracles *can* happen when you give yourself unreservedly.

I spoke of what happened once in the marketplace in my home town. There the story was constantly being repeated of the two people who met and knew immediately that they loved each other. The story of undisguised love.

But I didn't tell him how close to myself it was, that it was really my own first encounter with love. I have never wanted to relate the tale before.

I hoped he would understand that the miracle had occurred again, in the meeting of himself and Mary.

I knew the pain. I didn't tell him that miracles of love are linked to the moment. They give no guarantees for the future.

28th March

When I opened the door and found the room empty, there was only one idea in my head: I must find her. I ran out of the house and through the streets. To no avail. I thought once that it was her coming towards me. I rushed forward in delight, only to be disappointed; the woman was a stranger and bore no resemblance to her at all.

I didn't give up. I walked the same streets over and over again.

My hopes were continually being raised, only to be dashed the next instant.

Mary has vanished without trace, in all likelihood fled from the town. My first thought was to set off in search of her, but

I don't know what direction she would have taken.

She has probably joined one of the many groups of traders who travel together from town to town. She might have been on the ship that left harbour yesterday.

How could I let her go at the very moment that I'd found her? I'm sickened by the self-centredness I've displayed over the last few days.

He called it hubris.

Last night I again sought solace in wine and the storyteller's company. I told him of my inner torment.

Does Mary believe that I considered her a whore even on that final night when she came to me in my bed?

Did I tell her what I felt: that in my eyes she was the pure and chosen one?

I don't know what she believed.

He tried to console me. It didn't help. Then he asked me to come to the marketplace the next day and listen to his story.

He wanted to tell me a tale about the miracle of love.

I went there today and sat down in the crowd around him. He was sitting on the ground cross-legged in perfect equilibrium. Yet I could see that within himself he was in turmoil. He had difficulty keeping his voice in the usual even range of his narrative style: that is, low-pitched, not letting himself be carried away by the drama of the story, yet holding the attention of the listener.

He told the story of the miracle in the marketplace. Now I understand what he had been trying to explain to me the previous evening. His tale coalesced with the one echoing in me, a tale of Mary and myself. It was the story of our love.

It may be that I'll never find Mary again, but I know now that I shall finish painting the picture of her in the church so that they'll never forget her.

I know I can do it, even though she has gone. For me she is still there; I can see her. She is already sitting in her usual place, the light is shining obliquely down from the window high up beneath the vaulted roof. Her face is radiating light towards me.

The Elders cannot prevent me painting her. They cannot see her.

The Wondrous Event in the Marketplace

This was the third story I listened to in the marketplace.

A woman loved a man so fervently that she stripped naked for him in the marketplace. It's true, it happened in my own home town; I was there and saw it with my own eyes.

She was quite young, but a woman all the same. Her eyes displayed both the wonder of a child and the decisiveness of a young woman. It was her body she undressed, but it was her soul we saw, all of us in the marketplace that day.

The marketplace in my town is no different from those elsewhere. Women go there to buy food and men to meet other men. News is passed by word of mouth, and so is gossip.

Three people have their fixed sites in the square; each has his own corner that no one else is allowed to use.

The storyteller sits on the west side. He comes every day at the fourth hour after midday. He brings a mat with him, which he unfolds on the ground and sits on cross-legged. By telling his stories he connects the here and now to everything that has gone before.

On the east side is the weatherman. He never sits down. He arrives in the marketplace and takes up his position in his corner when the sun is at its highest. He proclaims his forecast standing. When it's done, he leaves immediately and is not seen again until the next day.

The weatherman, like the storyteller, enjoys great respect in the town.

But the one who is respected most of all is the wise man. He also sits on a mat, and his corner is on the north side. He can be found sitting immobile on his mat even before the sun rises, and he is still there when it sets.

Everyone who needs advice goes to the wise man. To him go the sick, or those who can't reach agreement with their neighbours. To him go fathers who want to marry off their daughters, or those who have lost their purses and cannot find them. For all of them he has an answer.

Nobody knows how old he is. His hair and beard are long, and his tunic worn into holes. He has been at his post for so many years that only the very oldest citizens can remember when he first arrived. Nobody knows where he came from, and he has no relatives here. His home is a shack outside the town.

The young woman knew the marketplace. She had been going there with her mother for as long as she could remember. At the beginning she was carried, later she walked with her hand clasped in her mother's.

Her parents were rich. The family lived in a large, elegant house with many servants. Nevertheless her mother went to the market every day herself to buy fresh produce.

She was the youngest daughter of the family. They loved her and gave her all their affection. They comforted her when she cried and laughed with her when she was merry. Afterwards, when everything had happened, there were many people who reproached them specifically for that.

"They've spoiled her," said one.

"A daughter should be brought up in modesty and obedience. Those are the virtues she needs when the day comes for her father to choose her a husband. They've filled her head with fancies instead," said another.

Perhaps people were right. If the couple had also had a son it might have been different. Then they would have realised how a daughter and future wife should be brought up. As it was, the little girl grew up with a strong will.

That was to prove disastrous when the time came for her first encounter with love.

He made his appearance on a perfectly normal day. She had gone to market with her mother as usual. She listened to the adults' conversations. The sun was shining. Then she saw him.

He was beautiful, and young, not much older than herself. His clothes and bearing indicated the confidence of the well-to-do.

Their eyes met as they passed. She knew at once. She cast her glance modestly down, but when she looked up again, he had gone. He had walked on in animated conversation with a friend and hadn't noticed her. She went back home with her mother in sadness and silence.

From then on she scanned the marketplace every single day for him. She went with her mother as before, but left her to be able to search more freely. A long time passed without her seeing him, and she returned home disappointed again and again. In the end she no longer knew whether he existed, or whether he was just a figure from a dream.

For she certainly had dreams.

In them he was miraculous. She could see him in the far distance. He would be approaching her with long, slow steps, his flowing dark hair swept back by the wind. He would be smiling and stretching out his arms towards her. He would call out something but she wouldn't be able to distinguish the words. Every time he would disappear before reaching her, and she would be left standing alone.

Finally one day she found him again.

He was seated in the crowd surrounding the storyteller, listening. She sat down too, with her head turned to observe him. She caressed his face with her eyes and fixed every feature in her memory. She sat undisturbed for some time, and then he flashed an angry glance at her. She was annoying him. He turned away, with a lowering expression, so that she couldn't see his face any more.

That evening she fell sick with a high temperature. She let it rage unresistingly. She couldn't tell the difference between night and day and no longer knew her parents.

Weeks passed before the fever subsided. She sat in a chair by the window for hours on end. But one fine day life reasserted itself in her young body. Her parents were filled with joy when they heard her laughter once more.

She had taken a decision, not just to live, but also to do something with her life. She went to the marketplace again with her mother.

When she got there, she went straight to the wise man's corner of the square. She found him alone and with his eyes closed. She hesitated, but then took the last few steps and sat down in front of him. She had often seen people do that when they came to him for advice. She also knew that when you did that, everybody else kept their distance. Both questions and answers would remain just between the two of them.

The old man sat there for a long time with his eyes closed. She didn't know whether he was asleep. Then he looked up and turned his gaze upon her.

"My child," he said, "what brings you to me?"

She bowed her head and blushed, but then plucked up courage and looked him straight in the eyes. In a low voice she told him of her love for the young man.

"What shall I do?"

The old man was silent; he pondered the matter before replying.

There was much talk later about the answer. Shouldn't he have told the young girl to go home to her father's house and wait there until he found a man for her? But the wise man didn't do that – he could see into the future and knew what was going to happen.

He smiled before he answered her:

"Show yourself to him, and he will see you."

That was all he said, and she knew that her time on the wise man's carpet had come to a close.

She went back to the marketplace the next day. She had been making herself ready since early that morning. She had bathed and washed thoroughly, dried her body and anointed it with oils. She chose her clothes with care and dressed slowly.

Her mother watched her preparations in amazement.

They went to the market together. And while her mother was busy with the shopping, the girl left her. She went in search of the young man and found him among a group of friends.

Without any hesitation she went up to him and forced him to look her full in the face. She saw his surprise and suspected his anger again. For a moment she wavered, her eyes no longer holding firm. But only briefly, and then she recovered again and returned his gaze defiantly.

What took place then would be recounted as a story for ever afterwards, over and over again.

With shy yet decisive movements she unfastened her clothes and let them fall to the ground. She slowly stripped naked for the man who stood there staring at her in alarm.

There was something touching in her performance, her movements were resolute but inexperienced, unhurried but not lingering.

In an instant consternation spread among the people. It swept like wildfire across the square and the crowd surged around the two of them.

Her mother rushed over, raising her arms to heaven and crying out in despair. Then she ran off in tears, cursing herself, her family and her daughter.

The excitement and clamour from the throng began to increase.

But for the young woman and man life stood momentarily still, just as long as it took for a miracle to occur. For that second they were entirely alone in the overflowing square. Everything and everyone ceased to exist.

They saw only each other.

Anger and fear melted away. He saw the naked woman standing in front of him. He saw her longing and knew that it was also his own. He accepted her undisguised love and was filled with infinite tenderness.

He fell on his knees before her, and then stood up again and covered her in his cloak, gathering up her clothes and leading her through the crowds with his arm around her.

The people gave way. They went completely quiet for the time it took the man to lead the woman away, across the square and out of sight. Then their voices rose anew.

They became a chorus of imprecation.

Nevertheless there were those who said immediately that it was a miracle they had witnessed. But most of them were outraged at the woman's shamelessness.

Surprisingly enough, by the very next day the mood had changed. Now there was a majority that admitted a miracle. Before the week was over, no one was in any doubt.

The girl's mother had run home and locked herself in. She was inconsolable – until the tales of the wondrous event began to reach her ears.

Then she too could see it was a miracle.

The couple left the marketplace in haste. He led her quickly to his house. They could have taken back ways out of sight of others, but chose to go by the main streets.

When they arrived, he lifted her up and carried her in. They stood in a close embrace and felt their pulses thudding.

The cloak slipped down from her shoulders. She let it fall, and didn't attempt to conceal her nakedness.

She stood naked before her beloved.

The story could have stopped here. But a further event occurred that amplified their tale and made it complete.

Some time had passed. The young couple were living together as man and wife. They spent all their time together, day and night. By day they sat beneath the trees in the orchard, by night they made love and slept in each other's arms. The love between them grew steadily deeper and more intense.

The young wife now went shopping in the marketplace herself, usually in the company of her husband. They both radiated joy.

But one day something occurred that threatened their happiness. A stranger came to the town. He took up position in the empty corner of the marketplace, on the southern side.

He called himself a storyteller, but he didn't follow the unwritten rules. He certainly told stories, but he wasn't satisfied with that. He drew a moral lesson from them and explained what was right and what was wrong.

Many people listened to him, even if no one liked him.

The stranger didn't believe in any miracle having happened to the young couple. He soon began condemning them from his corner. It was the woman in particular who deserved the admonition of the Lord.

His words had an effect on the populace. Firstly on those who hadn't been present when the miracle took place and thus hadn't seen it with their own eyes. And gradually his venomous words also seeped into those who had witnessed it.

One day the couple came to the square to shop. As usual everyone gathered around them.

Then the stranger pushed through the crowd towards

them. He was no longer content to voice his opinion from his own pitch. Once again he broke the rules: a storyteller should be sought out by those who want to hear him, and never force himself upon them.

People moved aside for his commanding figure. A space was made, and in it stood the man and woman before the stranger.

In stentorian tones he condemned them. Not the man, but the woman. She had offered her sex for sale in the market-place, just like a trader selling his wares.

The crowd's anger was inflamed. There were still some voices speaking out against the self-appointed judge, but they died away.

It was the words of the chastiser that moved the people and had the greater effect.

The miracle was forgotten, as was the emotion that had flowed through them all at the time it happened.

They saw it now through the stranger's eyes: the woman was unworthy, a whore who deserved her punishment.

She must be punished.

The young woman hid her face in her hands. She who less than a year ago had stood with uplifted head and stripped naked for her beloved, lowered it now and wept.

Someone looked for the first stone.

But her husband stepped forward. He struggled falteringly for words, but could find none. He too had a feeling of guilt; in some inexplicable way it had also reached the husband's mind, like a poison.

He could find no words. He stood quite still, his misery evident on his face.

Then he raised himself to his full height and looked the stranger in the eyes. He turned towards his beloved. Slowly he undressed. He unfastened one garment after another and let them fall to the ground. Finally he stood naked before her, naked too in the radiance of his gaze.

As he stood there, he was filled with a burgeoning love. The blood surged through his veins, filling his member till it rose and pointed upwards at an acute angle from his naked body.

It swayed in triumph.

He stood unclothed before his beloved, and she thrilled at the sight.

He paid no heed to his clothes on the ground. With his rigid member swinging before him he put his arm around his wife.

Together they walked off across the marketplace without a single person raising a hand or voice against them.

29th March

I am still looking for Mary, but without a hope of finding her. I've been down to the harbour and made enquiries there. No one can recall having seen a young woman with a child.

I wake up in the middle of the night weeping. By day I'm seized by an overwhelming restlessness. I have to go out in the streets to search for her. There's only one place where I can find any peace, and that's in the marketplace among the crowd gathered around the storyteller. I go there every day now and listen to his stories. In the evenings I seek out his company in the tavern. The wine has a numbing effect.

If a traveller comes to the inn, I ask him too. Has he met any groups on his way, and was there a woman among them?

Nobody has seen Mary or heard of her.

I think the time has come for me to go back to the church again.

29th March Continued

Light at last. I have been in the church and seen the painting. For a long time I didn't dare. What had I painted?

Would it be the whore staring at me from the picture, a reflection of my own inner turmoil?

God be praised, I have not been blind, I have painted her through His eyes. I didn't see her soul, but I painted it.

As yet I still cannot finish the painting. There is a fear inside me that must be conquered. It will be the test of myself as painter. Mary isn't here, she's no longer sitting on the stool in front of me, but I shall be able to see her.

God will help me when I myself am ready.

I went to the marketplace to listen again today.

What I had long suspected was confirmed. The storyteller is hiding behind a feigned serenity. Beneath the surface he is an unhappy man. His wounds have not healed. He is no longer telling stories to show me the world. They're all concerned with himself now.

The artist was ashamed. He admitted his shame and was liberated from it. He decided to paint it into his picture.

What did I do with *my* shame? I suppressed it for all these years. It lies hidden in my despair.

I realised that it was time to move on and confront the past. I have begun to gather my strength to face my own cowardice.

He has helped me. I thought I told the story of the young woman who stripped naked in the marketplace to console him or to help him to complete the painting of the Madonna and Child. But that wasn't the case.

It was myself I was obsessed with the whole time. And yet

I was still so far away from the point where I could openly admit my own shame or despair to myself.

The pain was going to become greater. The next day I went to the marketplace to tell the story of the youth who loved his aunt.

Temptation

This was the fourth story I heard in the marketplace.

A young man looked at his aunt one day and knew that he loved her. Not in the way a boy should love his aunt. No, he desired her as a woman.

"When a man's desire is awoken, there is no way to restrain it," the storyteller said, gazing around searchingly at his listeners.

"And," he went on, "if the man is also young and inexperienced, only providence can save him. Most often in the person of a woman, but occasionally also that of a man," he added slowly.

He regarded the group of adolescent boys around him and his eyes probed the young faces that were flushed with blood beneath the skin. For a moment their eyes sought his, as if in a forlorn attempt to prise a secret from him. The blushes betrayed their youth. Their blushes and their breathing. In young bodies breath, like blood, comes in spasms. In their vulnerability they revealed their own unconscious desire, while in shame and desperation they tried to conceal it.

It was with a painful tenderness that the storyteller surveyed his audience. He recognised their hidden distress, now so clearly revealed. Perhaps he was recalling the way it would come at night to a young man in his bed, how it came in a dream, like the caress of a gentle summer breeze yet also like a wild horse galloping across the fields. As both a promise and a demand, but above all as a storm of emotions without rhyme or reason.

Like an unintelligible madness, I thought, remembering. At that moment a sad smile passed over the storyteller's face. It seemed as if he had been brought up short by an old, young thought.

He recovered his voice and continued his tale. But the words came hesitantly, like the steps of an ageing traveller moving through a landscape he has only seen with youthful eyes.

His chosen love still had the deportment of youth, although she was nearly old enough to be the young man's mother.

She was pretty, and cared for her beauty in a discreet but nevertheless eye-catching way. She dressed simply, but her clothes hugged her body as if in affirmation. Not to the extent of being provocative, but so that all her movements were visible beneath the folds of cloth.

The boy observed all this one day when his aunt and uncle came to visit and the family were sitting together out in the garden. He observed more than that. He saw the wind ruffling her hair, loosening a lock and playing with it. He saw that she enjoyed the wind's caress, even when it tugged at her clothes and tricked its way inside. He saw that she reciprocated the caresses without moving, just by accepting them. He thought he could see a secret smile in her eyes.

Then he suddenly knew that he loved her, and the answers emerged from within himself to all his confused thoughts, to the unintelligible madness that had flooded through him in his lonely bed at night. The senselessness had gone, but the madness remained in his body, even stronger than before, transformed into desire, directed towards this woman in the sun and the wind, so familiar and yet so unknown to him.

He was bewildered. For it wasn't a single string vibrating within him, but a cacophony of notes. His desire contained tenderness, a wish to be intimate and close, to touch and give pleasure, a wish to be touched, to let things happen. But he knew it was more, an ungovernable urge, a compulsion to possess, to force his will.

These incoherent thoughts, or rather emotions, raced uncontrollably through the young man's mind as he sat there with his parents and siblings, his uncle and his aunt.

The storyteller shook his head slowly and was silent for a while before continuing. Could I not detect a slight but persistent quaver in his voice as he spoke? A tremor that revealed a personal connection to this story? And following his eyes, I couldn't help noticing how they shone when he described the woman.

None of the youths round the storyteller will ever be able to confirm that. They didn't dare look at him while he was speaking. But when he paused, they hesitantly turned their faces towards him. In their eyes the storyteller could read his own story as if in a mirror: at that moment they *were* the young man who saw his aunt and desired her.

The storyteller was silent for a little longer, then he cleared his throat and continued:

You can imagine how close the young man came to giving himself away. There and then. With his parents and siblings and uncle and aunt. He was full of new, tempting and frightening emotions, and he hadn't yet known the strength of desire. That it has to be curbed as much as it must be let loose. That there is a time for longing and a time for loving. He would become fully acquainted with the time for longing in the days and nights to come.

But at this very moment, with a newly discovered desire in his body, things went almost irretrievably wrong.

It was his aunt who saved him from disgrace. She must have perceived the pent-up agony in his young body, she had noticed the tension and she relieved it by knocking over her glass. The contents landed on her skirt and spread in a large wet stain. The sight of the broadening patch had an even more disturbing and immediate effect on the young man. He saw how the wine made the delicate fabric cling to the woman's flesh and reveal the contours of her thighs and loins.

Nevertheless he was saved. In the general upheaval that followed, the tension in his own body relaxed. Loud merriment arose in the hectic salvage operation, water and cloths were fetched, the stain was removed and assurances were exchanged that everything would quickly dry in the sun and wind.

No one else had noticed the boy's distress. No one other than the woman herself, his chosen one. There was a smile again in her eyes. That night he lay on his bed tossing and turning restlessly. The world had become a different place since he had risen that morning. He tried repeatedly to visualise his aunt in his mind, tried to conjure up her naked body. Finally he fell asleep in exhaustion. He dreamed of a large wet patch that spread and spread. It was there when he woke up.

The young man was in a state of confusion. Sometimes happy in his daydreams, sometimes dejected when the day pulled the carpet of dreams from under him. Days and nights came and went. To all appearances he led his normal life, continued his education, played with his friends. But he took no delight in it any more.

He knew that he would see his aunt again sooner or later, he dreamed of it, of their meeting, just the two of them, and that the world around them would be empty of people.

He met her in the market, where it was swarming with people. He met her in the very place where peace and quiet are banned from sunrise to sunset. She was buying fresh vegetables and putting them into a large basket. They suddenly stood before one another with no forewarning, staring each other in the face. A feeling of defiance rose in him, and he was determined not to lower his eyes. He succeeded, but he could sense his whole body stiffening. He tried to say something, but his tongue wouldn't obey him.

She averted her gaze and smiled, this time with her mouth. A strange smile, he thought later, as he cast his mind back over the meeting when he was alone again. She said something to him, but he didn't hear it, partly because of the noise of the marketplace, partly because all his energies were concentrated on the fact that his aunt was standing there, just one step away from him.

He stared at her as if turned to stone. Speechless. He could see that she was laughing and shaking her head and moving her lips, but not a word reached him. Only when she lifted up the basket of vegetables to the level of his eyes did he realise that she was asking him to carry it. He took hold of the basket, but his hand also grasped hers as she still held the handle. He let go as if burnt by fire. And there was the basket lying upside-down on the ground.

His body no longer paralysed, he bent down among the crowds of people and picked up the vegetables. Still in that position, he threw back his head and looked right into his aunt's face. She had crouched down too and was following his swift movements. Now he was holding the handle, and she was the one who put her hand over his and gave it a gentle squeeze. She smiled again, before quickly standing up.

They left the marketplace. He carried the basket for her.

She chatted as they walked, asked after his parents and his little brothers and sisters. He answered her questions, rather briefly and abruptly. He was struggling with himself the whole time to find something to talk to her about, but he couldn't think of anything. A silence fell between them. It was almost with relief that he saw they were standing outside his uncle's and aunt's house.

She put out her hand for the basket, and thanked him for his help. What thoughts passed through *her* mind when her hand again touched his? She doubtless felt the sweet temptation in herself, but had she even then decided what she wanted to happen? Perhaps it was at that moment that she gave herself up to fate.

She conveyed her greetings and disappeared into the house. He ran home through the streets, closed his door, threw himself on his bed and wept. Never, he thought, will I be able to free myself from my love.

But a week later fortune smiled upon him. The hunting season had arrived. He stood outside the house with his mother and brothers and sisters and waved goodbye to his father and uncle who were riding out of town in high spirits with a crowd of grown men. He suddenly felt glad that he wouldn't be old enough to join them until the following season. Earlier that summer he had been nagging his father for permission to go this very year. But his father had been adamant. "There's an age for everything," he said, "and next year you'll be old enough for hunting."

He didn't go to his aunt's house that day. He set out several times, but his courage failed him. But after a sleepless night he finally made a decision and found himself in front of her door. Still he hesitated, before eventually knocking cautiously. Not a sound was heard from the house. He knocked again, louder, and heard steps inside. Again he felt a kind of paralysis, and a flush that rose up like a sudden puff of hot air.

The door opened and she stood there before him, with a smile on her face. She bade him welcome, invited him in and locked the door behind them.

The storyteller fell silent again. He remained seated and motionless, with a faraway look in his eyes, in the circle of young men. He hardly seemed aware of them; it was probably memories that were running as tears in his eyes. He had no more to say.

The disappointment was tangible.

"Is that the end?"

The shadows on the marketplace had lengthened, the sun was dipping below the mountains in the west. Stallholders were raising their voices in one last frantic effort before everything went quiet in the darkness that was creeping over the square and town.

"No," said the white-haired storyteller, "it's not the end. As long as we live nothing is ever finished, even if we wish it were.

"That episode in the person's life was important when it happened, so it will never become unimportant for him as long as he lives.

"But what happened next between the youth and his aunt is a secret between those two people. That's how they wanted it, and that's how it shall be."

Then he really fell silent at last. The young men sat there for a while longer, also in silence, and then got up and disappeared across the square and into the night.

But the storyteller's eye fell on a boy who had stayed behind in the semi-dark. I was sitting somewhat outside the circle, already swallowed up by the shadows.

He noticed the lad's defiance, but also his unsureness. He motioned with his hand for him to speak.

"What shall I do?" the youth asked, his defiance even audible in his voice.

"I can't give you any advice," the storyteller replied. "Love has many stages. In the time of desire it takes no advice."

"But what did *you* do?"

The question had been put. Hardly out of interest in the storyteller's own fate, but because the youth's desire was raging within him and demanding an answer.

The storyteller pondered for a moment; I could sense him weighing up the questioner before he finally came to a decision and replied:

"I shall tell you. The night I came back from the hunt, a day before the others, and found my wife and the young man asleep in each other's arms, my world collapsed."

30th March

We met at the inn last night like brothers.

We said nothing before the wine was on the table. Then I asked:

"What did you do?"

He looked at me before he answered:

"I was seized by a terrible anger and raging jealousy. For one dreadful moment the urge to give free rein to my bitterness was almost irresistible. But I left the house with the sleeping couple in it. That night I was in hell. I roamed around aimlessly. Without a clear thought in my head I unhitched my horse and rode out of town.

"That's how I ended up here in this town, after travelling for weeks.

"I loved my wife, but I couldn't ever meet her again."

I sensed there was a lot he hadn't told me, but I left him in peace. We both carried a burden of sorrow, and both of us had revealed it. But whereas I wanted to talk of Mary constantly, he said not another word about his wife.

Nevertheless his unhappiness was plain to see, and I knew that he needed company. He downed the wine with the unnoticing carelessness of habit, but he showed no sign of intoxication. The wine had no effect on him.

He wanted to talk about the picture I was painting, and whether I'd resumed work again.

I told him that I'd finally plucked up the courage to return to the church to look at the picture, and of my relief on seeing it once more. How Mary shone out at me in her purity, the way I had perceived her. I admitted what my worry had been: that the painting might have revealed something else about myself, that I had known about her and painted a whore from the very beginning.

I confided my problem to him: the painting is almost finished, yet I feel that something essential has to be altered.

I have painted Mary against a blue background, as I decided at an early stage. I wanted thus to emphasise her purity. But it hasn't turned out as I expected. It was he, the storyteller, who had helped me. I told him so.

"You have opened my eyes," I said, raising my glass to him. "That's the way it is, it's debasement and suffering that creates purity in a person. Innocence that is only the result of inexperience has to be lost on the journey through life."

He responded to the toast with a shrug of the shoulders and we drank in silence.

"That's why I have to change the background in the painting. It has to depict evil."

The storyteller gave me a quick glance and took another drink before speaking.

"I can help you there too. I have made the acquaintance of evil. In myself as well as in others, not least here in this town. You've met the leader of the Elders. As a moneylender he has steadily built up more and more power over the years. With the signatures of many of the citizens on bonds of all sizes, he directs the town according to his own whim.

"He hasn't been elected Chairman of the Elders on the basis of confidence. It's fear that paved his way. I'll tell you a story now. It's about evil.

"What occurred just a few years ago should have led to the loss of everyone's respect for all time. But that's not how it turned out. For a while everyone laughed at him, but now the story merely serves to boost his power."

Evil

This was the fifth story I listened to. For obvious reasons the storyteller couldn't recount it in the marketplace, not in this town. Besides, it wasn't ready to be told publicly anywhere. Something was missing from it, he said, something that only time could complete.

A man owed so much money that he had to hire out his wife to pay his debts.

The matter only became widely known when it was all over. It was the dramatic ending that brought it out into the open and aroused the anger and imagination of the townsfolk.

The moneylender was quickly exonerated from any responsibility. Moneylenders usually are. They have a strange power over people, even over their opinions.

The general feeling was that he was simply running his business. If the money can't be recouped by any other means, then he ought to be able to collect it in pleasurable ways without risking life and limb.

The borrower, on the other hand, was accorded little respect.

Many people were interested in other aspects of the affair apart from the purely financial. There were titillating elements that had a secret appeal, especially for the men. Evil elements.

The moneylender was a short man, and over the years he had become stout. "There's something slightly licentious about him," it was often said. He was unmarried and lived a solitary life in the finest house in town. As a moneylender he was used to malicious gossip about himself. It didn't bother him. He had become as thick-skinned as his business required.

The borrower was a young, inexperienced businessman of good family. His father had built up his business into a substantial company. When he died, his son inherited everything and wanted to expand it further. Unfortunately he hadn't equipped himself particularly well for the task.

But he had achieved one thing: he had married a woman who was not only young and unusually pretty, but also had a cheerful disposition and a loyal heart. It was she who got her husband to change course.

He loved his wife and took up the management of the family firm with great diligence and spirit.

It would soon prove not to be enough. The son was far from stupid, but he lacked experience. He realised this, but thought it not so important because he had his father's most trusted assistant at his side, who had been the father's right-hand man for many years and knew all about the business. Now he was to help the son learn. But he was far from pleased about that: he had entirely different plans for the future.

The assistant didn't let his bitterness show, nor his covert desire for things to go badly for the son.

On the contrary, he was always ready to offer advice. It was just that the advice was never good enough, and it was said afterwards that he also stole money from the firm. Be that as it may, he certainly had enough funds on the day the young owner had to close down the company, and was able to acquire it for himself.

But before matters got that far, the young man had been struggling hard for several years. One day at the end of the first year, while a travelling salesman was standing there with his wares waiting for payment, the assistant had coughed humbly and said they had no money. The matter was promptly settled; he had dealt with the firm over many years and was happy to give credit.

The young owner was saved, but was well aware that the reprieve was only temporary. He would soon have to face the problem again.

It was at that point that he asked his assistant for the advice that was to prove his undoing.

"Large companies quite often run low on cash nowadays," the assistant said. "It's not uncommon at this time of year when travelling salesmen arrive. You can take a short-term loan, it's a perfectly normal thing to do."

The young man grasped the salvation offered.

"Who can lend me money?" he quickly asked.

The assistant hesitated momentarily before mentioning the moneylender's name. He needn't have worried. The owner was inexperienced, and it meant nothing to him. It should have done.

The very next day he was knocking at the moneylender's door. The young man was well prepared, he knew how important it was to create an impression of reliability.

He spoke about his business in detail and at length, as he had been advised by his assistant. He gave an account of the products, their prices and qualities. He listed suppliers and customers. He gave an overview of the value of the stocks and orders. He was careful to mention that there had never been any significant reduction in customer numbers.

The moneylender asked one or two questions from time to time, to augment his understanding of the situation. He gave the appearance of following attentively, but the potential borrower had the feeling that his mind was elsewhere.

The young man finished by setting out his present seasonal need for a loan.

There was silence. He shifted uncomfortably in his chair. The moneylender had listened impassively but was clearly enjoying the situation.

"Good," he said finally. "You can borrow the money, on the usual terms." He outlined what they were, in a succinct and professional manner. The interest rate and repayment frequency were as the assistant had suggested, so the young man simply nodded in relief and accepted it all.

"Then there's just one other thing. It's really a pure formality, a curiosity that's remained in the loans business since time immemorial," the moneylender said with a short, rather forced, laugh, which the young man, in his euphoria, didn't notice.

"In the promissory note there's a clause to the effect that the lender can, in case of default, demand one of the borrower's limbs instead.

"A pure formality," he added hastily. "I can't remember a single occasion when the condition has been enacted."

It's easy to say afterwards that of course the young man should have said no, that he shouldn't have accepted the loan on these terms. It's equally easy to say he shouldn't have taken a loan at all, but should have wound up the company immediately. But someone who's fighting to keep a business alive doesn't think like that. He just imagines that if he could only have a little breathing space now, he can put things right, that he'll have saved the whole enterprise before the day of reckoning.

Those were indeed the young man's thoughts. He nodded his acceptance again.

So the moneylender drew up the details of the agreement. He wrote out the promissory note with a practised hand, dried the ink and handed it to the borrower.

"Read it carefully," he said, "so that we can be sure we're agreed on what's written."

With a clap of his hands he summoned his servant to witness the signature.

The young man picked up the promissory note and felt his hand shaking. He read the text, but his mind was no longer concentrating. It suddenly had but one single object: to get the matter completed. He inscribed his signature.

The moneylender took the document and passed it to his servant, who signed as witness.

On a separate table in the office there stood a chest furnished with a strong lock. The moneylender solemnly unfastened it and counted out the money in gold. Then the promissory note was placed in the chest and it was securely locked again.

When the owner returned, his assistant was waiting to hear whether the loan had been successfully negotiated. What kind of conditions had been imposed? He described the repayment time and interest rates, but didn't mention the personal security the moneylender had demanded.

Nor did he do so when he told his wife that same evening about his application to the moneylender and reassured her that all their problems were now over.

Far from it. Not many weeks had elapsed before his assistant again came to see him about the lack of money for running expenses.

From then on events moved quickly, and to a familiar pattern. For a while the money shortage is noted, but the situation is kept under control. Then the problems become more insoluble. Suppliers become impatient and eventually suspicious. In the end they are afraid of not getting their money. Then it's not long before they are all demanding payment at the same time.

In desperation the young man sought the only way out he could think of. Once again he knocked on the moneylender's door. But the moneylender was a professional. He was still friendly, but very firm. Half an hour later, the man was back on the street without any new loan, but with a polite reminder that their settlement of account would soon fall due.

Bad times followed. On settlement day he was again standing in the moneylender's office. The promissory note was laid before him. The moneylender was angry, he had never actually experienced this before, but he was obliged to collect his security. As a matter of principle.

The debtor did not, however, bear himself as an abject coward. He had thought the matter over carefully. The promissory note had plagued him like a nightmare for many sleepless nights. He realised now that the terrible clause was rather more than a formality and that he couldn't expect any mercy.

He had accepted it. The young man felt that he had fought a good battle and overcome his fear.

He stood before the bondholder pale but composed. He calmly rolled up the sleeve on his left arm, held it out, and told the moneylender to take his pledge. But the latter simply looked at him in surprise.

The young man was suddenly frightened. Had he misunderstood something?

A moment later the ghastly truth dawned on him. The moneylender held up the promissory note and read the terrible clause aloud to his victim:

"The borrower puts up as security for the loan one of his limbs, at the lender's choice, which is to be severed in default of payment."

He did not want the young man's left hand.

"No," he said, with a hint of a smile, "that would be getting off too cheaply. Since the choice is mine, I would like your male adornment, your nocturnal implement, if I may attribute so fine a name to your member."

The young man's new-found calmness ceased abruptly. The cruel demand hit him with paralysing force. He besought the moneylender for mercy, on his knees before him. With an angry movement the bondholder freed himself from the wretched man's grip on his trouser leg.

He took a few steps across the room before speaking. It was

important for him to stress the nature of his own predicament. He was the one who was the injured party. He had lent out his money in good faith, and now it was lost. And if that wasn't enough, he was now forced, out of regard for his principles, to undertake a painful debt collection. So he had a right to expect that the other party show a degree of honour and keep to the clearly stated terms of the contract.

The young man still begged for mercy. Anything but that. He would do anything at all for the moneylender, only not that.

The old man wrung his hands in feigned dismay; he wanted his victim to squirm a little longer. How could he trust him, he asked.

"Try me," the young man implored, and was lost.

Now the moneylender changed tack. He adopted a friendly voice and asked the poor man to sit down.

"I think we can find a way out of this unfortunate situation," he said. "With good will on both sides, it should be possible."

For a moment the victim took heart.

"You have a young and beautiful wife," the moneylender continued. "I've often seen her in the marketplace, to my great delight."

There was a short pause.

"I have a proposal to settle our account. Your wife can pay your surety for you by coming to me at my house. She must do so one hundred times, on the last day of the week, after nightfall.

"You know the going rate for that kind of work. If you do the calculation and bear in mind that I ought to have a little interest on my money, I'm sure you'll find the arrangement reasonable for both of us."

The moneylender propounded his suggestion in a considered fashion hardly indicative of sudden inspiration.

The young man saw the extent of his misfortune, and realised that the moneylender had been playing with him from the very first day. He stared at him helplessly for a moment, and then was seized with rage; but the servant was there immediately to hold him fast.

"Our discussion is over," said the moneylender. "My proposal is straightforward. If it's accepted, we don't need to meet again. If, on the other hand, you decline it, we must meet once more so that I can collect my dues. I await your response on the last day of next week."

The businessman came home feeling nauseous, and refused to eat for several days. At night he would scream out in nightmares, and by day he lay silently staring at the ceiling. His wife tended him lovingly night and day. Nevertheless, he couldn't bear her near him, and if she touched him he would turn over in irritation.

On the last day of the week he could defer it no longer. He concealed his desperation and his fear and in an astonishingly cool and detached manner told her of the dreadful situation.

Unable to say more, he sat there looking at his horror-stricken wife. He didn't know where his own wretchedness ended and hers began. Were they hers or his, those repulsive images of the moneylender fondling her with his lustful hands? Pressing his engorged sexual organ against her in breathless arousal and forcing his way into her and squirting his seed into her womb?

The young man didn't know, because she was silent. He put his arms around her, wanting to hold her tight, but now it was she who rejected him.

At sunset she got herself ready and went out. She turned in the doorway and looked once more at her husband. It was as if she were still hoping she had misunderstood, that he would call to her and prevent her going.

He ran to her at once and embraced her. Then, scarcely

realising what he was doing, he pushed her out into the encroaching dusk.

She stood before the man who had bought her one hundred times. She didn't make it easy for him when he welcomed her. He poured out wine, but she didn't touch it. And when he stood before her, with his naked, ageing body, she laughed mockingly at him and spat. She saw him growing angry and was glad. He tore the clothes off her.

She lay there in anguish listening to the breathing of the sleeping man spread half across her body. She freed herself cautiously and sat up. She looked down at the sleeping face. Sleep had erased the anger and lust, but the evil could not be so easily scoured from his dissolute features.

Then she saw the servant standing motionless at the foot of the bed.

She went to the moneylender's house every week for two years. She no longer spat as she had done the first time. She drank from the glass he handed her, and at a sign from him she undressed. She even learned to tolerate the presence of the servant.

She answered his questions, but asked none herself. The moneylender tried giving her presents to ingratiate himself with her. An expensive ring or a wonderful necklace. She received them from him, but left them lying there when she went.

At home she was almost as she had always been. Her husband wanted to think so. They shared a bed. The wife saw to the house, if anything more thoroughly than before. They never talked about it.

The two years passed, and the woman had been to the moneylender for the hundredth time. She came home and handed over the promissory note. Her husband embraced her.

A week passed. On the last day of the week she got ready

again at sunset. Her husband stared at her in dismay. She pushed him aside without a word, and before the dumbstruck man had time to react she went off into the night.

It was the servant who opened the door. Totally expressionless, he showed her in to a bewildered moneylender. She stood there. She talked. And laughed. She drank up her wine and asked for more. She went up close to him and unfastened his clothes. He received this new woman in amazement. He willingly dismissed the servant. In bed she gave him joy and satisfaction.

That night she got out of bed and looked down at the sleeping man. His member lay slack between his legs after their union. She lifted it carefully with one hand. With a knife in the other she swiftly severed it from his body. The screams from the de-sexed man followed her out in her flight from the house.

She was sought everywhere in the days that followed, but she was never found. A salesman who visited the town annually said some years later that he had met a woman in a brothel in a distant town who exactly resembled the young businessman's beautiful wife. No one was ever able to confirm the traveller's assertion. Neither of the men in the story came out of it with honour. The moneylender didn't need it. He had his power. And the woman hadn't been thorough enough – the man lost his member, but retained his lust. It was soon said that he still took delight in tricking young and preferably married women into coming to him.

He also invested an increasing passion into the moneylending business. He gained a perverse pleasure from entrapping unfortunate people in his web. He let them wriggle while he exploited them.

So it was that he was elected Chairman of the Council of Elders and held all the strings in his hands. And if the truth be told, the town flourished under his leadership.

The unhappy husband lost his manhood in a less bloody, but nevertheless more shameful, way. He faced a tragic future.

31st March

I was seized yesterday by the most horrible feeling, like a cold claw gripping me around the heart, while I was still sitting in the tavern listening to the story of the town Elder. It hadn't let go when I was walking home through the dark night. I felt as if I was being followed by evil eyes.

Heavy and drowsy from the wine, I fell asleep quickly, but not into a tranquil slumber. I dreamed that I was in a snake pit, with slippery snakes squirming all around me in their hundreds. I was staring into red snake eyes, mesmerised, unable to move.

I was woken by my own screams, shaking and wet with sweat. I lay there awake, still trembling with fear.

After a while I slid into a dreamy state again. But the vision of the glistening, writhing mass of snakes wouldn't go. In my sleep, yet nevertheless consciously, I could feel my own body taking on the form of a snake. Wet with slime, it pushed its way through the coils of living bodies. In a state of terrified frenzy I could feel my fear being slowly replaced by the excitement of lust. The contractions of my stomach turned into rhythmic thrusts in time with a thousand other bodies.

Now I was no longer a snake in a snake pit. I was a money-lender, being visited by a woman. I undressed her lingeringly. She let it happen. My hands fondled her body, greedily demanding, consumed by desire. Possessing. Beside myself with lust I forced her beneath me and took her. Brutally, and yet enjoying it, I grasped her under the chin and turned her averted face towards me and stared into her eyes in savage triumph.

It was Mary.

1st April

I'm not going to the tavern today. I'm not going out, I can't look people in the eye. After the terrible deeds of the night I collapsed on my bed like a corpse. I slept without dreaming till far into the next day. I returned to consciousness only reluctantly. I couldn't admit even to myself what had happened. I can still feel the grip of lust within me; how easy it would be to let it take hold again.

My exposure was so simply accomplished. He knew what he was doing, the storyteller, when he told the tale of the moneylender and the woman. He must be laughing at me and my incessant worry about purity. He saw through me and wanted to show me my true face.

He has succeeded.

2nd April

I went to the tavern after all. He was sitting there in his usual place and bade me welcome.

He said not a word to indicate that anything might have occurred.

He listened uncomprehendingly to my first mumbled words while I was still standing at the foot of the table. He beckoned me to sit down on the bench, called for a jug of wine for me and pretended that everything was normal.

I couldn't go on, I had to have it out with him. It came tumbling forth like an incoherent confession of sins, completely muddled; he had to hear it all, the whole of my despicable snake-like existence.

He let me talk, waited until I had given vent to all my despair. He didn't say much then, either. But his eyes still looked sad as he raised his glass with a wry smile and drank.
"That's the way we are," he said. "Think yourself lucky that it's only in your dreams that your evil self appears."

He sat quietly for a while. Was he on the point of saying something about himself?

"Evil is part of man's nature, so it can also be forgiven," was all he said.

"It's when it's combined with hubris that it's unforgivable," he added.

The wry smile was still on his face, like an ironical sneer, directed against himself.

3rd April

It was late by the time I left the tavern. The candle had burned down and been replaced by a new one. My wine glass had been emptied and refilled many times. I no longer felt my own despair to be so threatening. His stories of the last few days were merging together and leaving me in a state of uneasy confusion.

When we finally rose to say goodnight, he looked at me and said again: "Think yourself lucky you're not driven by hubris."

Safely back home in my lodgings, I fell to my knees and prayed fervently to God for forgiveness for my evil thoughts. That gave me peace. I slept soundly, and woke today with a wondrous feeling of certainty.

I can go back to the church again and the picture of Mary. I know how I'm going to finish it. I don't need to seek out the evil in others in order to paint the background. I have my own, an evil I didn't think I knew. To me it's like colours on a surface wash of sin. Simply through painting I will at last be able to acknowledge the evil within myself and make my peace with God.

4th April

The picture is finished. I have painted the background as if in a fever. At last there is nothing else I want to change. Everything is as it should be. I know that it's good. I would have liked to have shown it to my old master and seen his nod of approval. Never before have I painted anything like this.

Now I will just sort out my affairs here in the town before I go on my way, to start my search for Mary.

134

6th April

This is written in great haste: in an hour's time I'll be on board the ship that will take me to Mary.

Last night she came to me in a dream. She was pale and serious and indescribably beautiful in her black dress.

"I know you want to find me," she said, "so go down to the harbour in the morning. There's a blue ship moored there, which will be sailing south. The captain is a short man, with the scar of a deep gash running from his left ear down to the corner of his mouth. Stay with that ship until you find me."

Before I could ask her anything, she was gone again. I was down at the harbour yesterday. I saw the blue ship, and the captain with the scar.

I went down there again early this morning and found the ship and its captain. He was ready to set sail for Ancona, but promised to wait while I fetched my things.

I won't have time to collect my fee for the painting. But I have enough money from previous commissions, and I'm glad I won't be standing before the Elders again. The woman who looks after the house here has promised to pass on the message that the painting is finished and that I have left.

I'll pack up my notes; they served their purpose while I was working. My hope is that you, storyteller, will ask after me. The woman has been told to hand over the papers to you. It's your stories I've written down, after all, and if I know you aright, you'll be able to make use of the notes about Mary for a new one.

I can still see the moneylender, the leader of the Council of Elders, as I stood before him. I had made contact with him in order to buy the painting. I saw his momentary astonishment, revealing both suspicion and triumph. I saw his flabby fingers curl round the gold chain hanging down over his portly stomach.

Suspicion, because it is an important item of equipment in all financial affairs.

Triumph, because he had already been struggling with the question of how to dispose of the picture. For almost any price, he'd thought to himself. Now he had his eye on the chance of a good profit too.

I was careful not to say what I knew when he was about to name a figure: that the artist hadn't received anything for his work because he had left town before he could collect the fee due under his contract. I didn't want to challenge the money-lender unnecessarily; I was too interested in the picture to risk that.

Nevertheless, I had set myself a limit. When I reached it without any sign of acceptance, I broke off the negotiations and took my leave. My calculation proved to be correct: the next day he sent a messenger with a letter. My offer was accepted, even though the town would bear a loss, the letter said.

Well, the picture was worth the sum I paid, and more besides. But at the same time I knew that the deal gave special pleasure to the Elders, the only pleasure they had had from the ill-fated experiences the painting had brought them.

It was hard to say goodbye to the landlord and his wife at the inn. The woman wept when I put my arms round her and kissed her. Even the landlord looked sad. He bade me farewell as if I were his dearest friend.

The Miracle

This is the night before I start on the last stage home, the three days' walk from this mountain village in the valley out to the Ligurian coast where the sea is in the west.

It's impossible to sleep. When I glanced into the church a short while ago I saw the priest at prayer up at the altar. A single candle cast a flickering light on the altarpiece.

It's two days since I came here. I've used that time to copy and sort the papers, mine and his. The artist's. But mainly I've been thinking over my situation and putting all my cards on the table in my own mind.

I arrived once before in this remote valley, ten years ago, when it was still night. I had been fleeing along mountain paths for three days. For most of the way riding was imposs-ible; I had had to steer both myself and the horse cautiously past the most treacherous abysses. Persistent wind and rain didn't make the journey any easier. The cold ate into the body and spread like a paralysis. I had been tempted to put an end to everything and pitch myself into the gorge below.

But I had struggled on. In the darkness I didn't see the little village with its low houses until I was right in the midst of them. They are built of stone without mortar. Only the church distinguished itself slightly from the other houses, even though it too was built of the same material. A cross on the gable dispelled any lingering doubt.

I was thoroughly chilled and shivering when I found the door. It was open.

Freezing and wet, I sought shelter in a corner. That was

how the young priest found me when dawn broke, numb with cold and despair.

He didn't ask any questions when he saw the exhausted wretch that I was. He took me to his little room next to the church, helped me off with my clothes, and gave me a coarse, tattered priest's habit to put on.

He made a fire and heated something to drink. I curled up by the fire. He shared his dry bread with me and filled a cup with wine, still without asking me anything. Soon I was lying on the priest's bed, and fell into a deep sleep.

When I woke again, it was night, a new night. I could just make out the priest, who had lain down on the floor in the chilly room with nothing over him.

My despair had set in again. What should I do? I knew that I couldn't return home. The prospect of facing my wife after what had occurred was unbearable.

I felt that everything had been taken from me, and I had decided to travel, to get away from it all.

Had I thought about the worry and uncertainty in which I had left my wife? Yes, I had. And I was glad. I wanted revenge. I wanted to know that she was suffering. For many years I believed in my right to act like that. Until I met the artist, in fact, whose naive belief showed me my own self-righteous arrogance.

On that one dark, desperate night, I had become a perpetrator of violence. Then I concealed my misdeed by setting myself up as judge. I condemned my wife to lifelong torment.

Is there forgiveness? I don't know, but it's to beg for forgiveness that I am making my way back home tomorrow.

I became quite close to the priest in those few days many years ago before I continued on my journey. He was young and a novice in his calling. I had told him what had happened; or rather, some of it. The part that had to do with the injustice I had suffered. He, and the artist, should have known what evil I was keeping secret. I, who allow myself to tell the story of the moneylender.

The priest chose his words carefully, but I remember him trying to get me to view my situation in a different and more positive light. He didn't see through me.

He himself had a very strong faith. He didn't regard his assignment to an impoverished mountain village as a banishment, but as a mission entrusted to him by God.

It's not a place one would willingly move to, a tiny collection of grey houses, ravaged by time and by the wind that seldom abates up there in the mountains.

The people are like the houses, grey and sad, and not particularly firm believers, according to the priest, very few of them attending church. Most of them needed solace in their monotonous, poverty-stricken lives, but they preferred to find it in the village's single tavern.

The priest didn't let himself be demoralised by the hopeless conditions, even though he obviously didn't have enough to eat. He was entirely dependent on the gifts he got from the local people.

"Things can only get better," he had said.

Coming back after ten years was quite a shock. As I stopped outside the church it looked even more wretched than before. I tapped on the priest's door, which was unlocked, but he wasn't there. The room was just as spartan, but now it seemed filthy and neglected. I couldn't find him in the church, either.

Back outside I stopped a passer-by and asked whether he knew where the priest might be found. A scornful smile crossed his solemn face:

"He's probably in the tavern."

I found him there in a corner, sunk down in the seat with an empty mug in front of him. He raised his head momentarily and saw me; then lowered it again and stared at the floor.

In that brief glimpse of his face I could discern the whole extent of his misery and debasement.

Gone was the priest's strong, youthful faith. His eyes were empty and unsteady, his features lined with hunger and disillusionment.

He explained how he was able to sit in the tavern drinking wine despite not having the means to buy food. The landlord had announced several years before that he would pay *his* contribution to the church, one jug of wine per day. But it had to be drunk in the tavern. It was meant as mockery, and was understood as such by the priest. Nevertheless, the starving and lonely man of the cloth had eventually gone to the tavern and accepted the wine. Since then he came every evening and emptied his mug. He sat in his corner and let their laughter ride over him.

I ordered a jug of wine and poured out some for us both. He grasped his mug and drank greedily. I realised that it was food he needed, and asked the landlord to set the table. The priest ate solidly without talking. I was afraid his starved stomach wouldn't be able to hold the food down.

It was a sorrowful tale he had to tell me. He related it all in shame: the story of the young priest who in his arrogance had thought he could achieve the impossible: win the people for God and make of the impoverished village a fortress of the spirit. He spoke of all his mistakes and humiliations, day by day, year after year, until now he just sat in the tavern and drank.

He wasn't making a secret of anything, not even his personal failure and defeat. He had managed to achieve nothing of what he had set out to do in his youthful enthusiasm.

He even thought he had lost his faith. He had not felt God's support for a single instant ever since he came to the church so many years ago.

I didn't offer him any advice, but asked whether I could stay with him for a few days. I told him a little of what had happened to me over the years since we had last met. We went together to the room at the church.

Now it was I who helped him into bed. He wanted to lie on the floor, as he had that time before, but in his drunken state he quickly complied and fell asleep immediately.

With the painting under my arm and a lighted candle in my hand I went into the church. I put the candle on the altar. Then I gently unwrapped the painting from its cloth cover. There in the faint light it looked more beautiful than ever. In this pitiful church, with no other ornament, the picture would in the future be the centre of attention.

A rough-hewn figure of Christ crucified hung above the altar. I lifted it down. There was a ring on the back of the statue to attach it to the hook in the wall. With some effort I managed to get it out.

Taking great care, I tried to fix it into the back of the painting. It was difficult without any kind of tool. I had to beware of damaging the picture. I gave up after several attempts and placed it on the altar, leaning against the wall. The priest could hang it up himself.

Then I raised the candle and let it shine on the painting again. It would have been a treasure in the most beautiful church on earth. Here it had found its place in one of the poorest and meanest houses of the Lord.

I put the crucified Christ down on the floor against the wall. I suspected that the priest had carved it himself, presumably in his early optimistic phase.

He's no artist, there's no doubt about that. Time will tell whether he's still a priest.

I went silently back to his room and lay down on the floor with my cloak over me. I wasn't very comfortable, but felt a powerful sense of calm seeping into me.

When I woke the next morning, the priest was gone. I

peered inquisitively into the church. He was on his knees in front of the altar deep in prayer. I left him in peace and tidied his little room instead. Then I set the table with food that I'd brought back with us from the tavern the previous night.

A long time passed before he returned. I heard his steps through the church and knew at once that what I'd hoped for had come about.

His eyes were radiant, even more so than when I'd first seen him. He had straightened himself up. He looked at me confidently, right into my eyes.

"A miracle has happened!" he exclaimed. "God has spoken to me. For the first time in all these years He has given me a sign."

He pulled me into the church and pointed up at the painting. He had fixed the ring and fastened the picture high on the wall. It hung there in daylight like a triumph of faith.

Not for a single instant did it occur to him to ask whether I had had anything to do with it. He had witnessed the inexplicable miracle and he believed. He didn't need to seek any rational explanation of how it had happened. He didn't want to seek one.

He wanted to believe.

A short while later an old woman entered the church, one of the few believers in the district. She too saw the miracle above the altar. That was how the news was carried out to the village.

Some hesitated to approach, but soon the church was full to overflowing. They wouldn't go until the priest had conducted a service. The people of the village bowed their heads and received the miracle with incomprehensible Latin words. The priest's chant could be heard faintly through the gaps in the walls of the church.

Then it suddenly seemed as if it was forcing its way out between the stone blocks and rising in thanks to heaven. At the beginning still cautious and tentative, but soon with increasing strength. And the congregation was singing too, the Latin words bursting forth and surging up in an ecstatic and mighty chorus.

And now something even more inexplicable occurred. The vibrating soundwaves converged and hovered above the congregation like a rainbow. The low roof was gone. The tones of the singing rose towards heaven, and the rainbow formed a vaulted arch on high. They saw it there momentarily before feeling it subside again and become part of their own singing.

Can I interpret that as a sign to me too? Is there forgiveness? How can I otherwise understand that a murderer can perform miracles?

The priest and his congregation are on their way towards happier times now. People came past the priest's door in the course of the day and evening. They left small gifts, mainly food. It wasn't very much from each individual – almost everyone up here is poor – but together it was enough for the priest for weeks to come. Even the wine from the tavern was brought to the door.

We sat up for many hours tonight. The priest is sleeping in his bed now, his face at peace like a child's. He stayed in the church praying at the altar for a long while after we had finished our conversation.

I myself want to complete my notes on everything that has happened before I go to sleep.

The Sacrificial Lamb

The priest had to keep on reminding us both about the miracle all evening. I could no longer find any satisfaction in his simple faith, the way I had in the church when the singing uplifted us all. I had gone back to that night ten years before, when I had knocked on the priest's door, wet and miserable.

What I have suppressed ever since, from myself and from others, is that when I came to the priest then it was as a murderer.

Now I finally summoned up my courage and asked the priest to listen to what I had to say.

I ran away from the house after finding my wife sleeping in the arms of another man, and roamed aimlessly about the town for hours in great agitation. I was filled with a numbing despair.

Then I mounted my horse and rode out of town. I had decided to stay in hiding until it grew dark the following evening. I wouldn't return until then, at the time I knew my friends would be coming home from hunting. I would maintain silence about what I knew.

When daylight broke, I stopped and let my horse graze in a meadow between the mountain crags. I remained in hiding all day, and saw not a single person the whole time. I was calmer again when I remounted my horse. The sun was sinking into the sea in the west.

It was dark before I reached town. I rode slowly through the empty streets and cut through the marketplace. The great fountain stood alone in silhouette. As I passed close by it, I became aware of a figure sitting on the stone steps, bent forward, head in hands.

I recognised him, even in the darkness. It was him. He looked up at that very moment, and his young, white face shone out at me.

I swear I had no evil intentions when I dismounted and went over to him. He had stood up. He recognised me too. He took a step towards me. Was there a nervous smile on his lips?

I remember nothing more, not until he was lying there as a lifeless bundle in a pool of blood. I had stabbed him again and again, transformed his lithe body into a dead mass, a corpse.

I can't remember it, yet I can recall the sight of his youthful, innocent face as I stabbed him the first time. His eyes registered astonishment and pain before they were extinguished.

In a single mindless instant, in uncontrollable rage, I had killed someone, an innocent human being. A young boy who had just begun his quest in life.

I was a murderer.

I was unable to look at the priest as I spoke. But I did so now. And what I read in his eyes was that he had not received my confession in God's service. He had taken it as the confidence of a friend. He could see that I was not ready to receive absolution.

Reassured, I carried on. I tried to describe the terrible moment when consciousness returned, as I bent over the dead boy with my dagger in my hand. I could no longer bear to hold it. But I didn't simply throw it away. It was a unique knife, the handle decorated with inset stones. If *that* was found near the body everyone would know who the malefactor was. I would have to dispose of it.

I was suddenly obsessed with the need to conceal the dagger. In feverish and random haste I searched for a hiding place. I discovered one. The fountain was constructed on a square pediment with steps on all four sides. The pediment consisted of carved stone blocks. In some places there were slight gaps between them.

On the east side of the fountain I encountered a gap that was larger than the others. I could get my arm in, right up to the elbow. That was where I hid the knife, and I felt a temporary sense of relief, until desperation set in once more.

I left the body lying where it was. It would be discovered the next morning. I would be far away by then. I could see the people now in my mind. Enraged, hunting frantically for the murderer. I thought too of the impossibility of facing my wife. Then, and for a long, long time, it was to her I attributed the guilt for the disaster.

Without having chosen any particular route, I found myself on the narrow path that I knew led up to the confined village in the mountains. It started to rain, which at first I experienced as a relief. Then the wind gradually increased, and the temperature up in the mountains dropped as night approached. The weather had turned against me.

Now here I sat, ten years after my crime, telling the priest what had really happened. He took my hands, and held them long and hard in his. He said not a word about what I had confessed. He didn't impose himself upon me. He didn't invoke God's name. He could see that this was the first time I had confronted my tragedy again, even for myself. And that I needed longer before I could seek and receive absolution. He knew that I had to go back the *whole* way first.

He remained silent and was there as a friend.

Tomorrow I shall continue my journey. I shall return home and meet my wife. I shall stand there openly. So first I must ride to the fountain and retrieve the dagger. From now on I shall conceal nothing of what I have done.

ROME 1989

The Dagger

I too have no desire to conceal anything. But the problem is that so much is concealed from myself. I can remember nothing of what I've done. The sentence of eight years' imprisonment was based entirely on the word of others.

My wife came home from the party at about three o'clock the night I sat up reading the manuscripts for the first time. I heard a car stop outside and leapt over to peer out between the curtains. Down below I could see my wife and a tall man getting out of the car. She kissed him lightly on the cheek and went straight to the door as she looked for her keys in her bag. The man stood there briefly watching her go in. Then he lit a cigarette, got into the car and drove off. Immediately after that I heard her open the door of the apartment.

She looked into the study, astonished to see me still up. When I asked if she'd had a good time, she gave a faint shrug of the shoulders and said: "Yes – not bad."

Without saying more, she kissed me good night and went into the bedroom. There was a smell of wine on her breath. I stayed up for another couple of hours and finished reading the documents. I am haunted by these figures from the past.

What happened to them? Did the painter ever find his Mary again? The fact that there weren't any other known pictures painted by the same artist might indicate that his life had been short.

And the storyteller – did he manage that last, difficult stage of his journey home to his wife? Did he find peace in his house, or did he go away again?

149

I couldn't follow him any further. His journey onwards from the little village in the mountains would remain in total obscurity.

But no, not entirely. There was one other element he had included – the dagger he had hidden in the pediment of the fountain.

I had very disturbed dreams when I eventually went to sleep for the few remaining hours of the night. I was myself, yet I was searching for Mary. I left port in a blue ship, only to discover with dismay that Mary was still standing on the jetty, waving to me.

She was attired in the same simple black dress that the artist had described, but when she called to me she had my wife's face. There were still only a few yards between the ship and the quay, yet I couldn't understand what she was saying. The ship slid inexorably away from land.

Then a figure came on to the quay behind Mary. He went close up behind her and put his arms round her. She turned her head, as if to see who was embracing her. Then I saw his face pressed against her pale cheek. It had the features of the bank manager. Now the distance between the ship and the jetty increased more swiftly and the two figures soon merged into one.

I screamed out, and sat up in bed with a start. I was gasping for breath, and dripping with sweat. Seconds later my wife was there. She held me in her arms and comforted me. She hummed a tune in a low voice and cradled me like a baby. I gradually calmed down again. Her arms, that had been holding me tight, loosened their grip and rested gently across my breast. I fell asleep again, this time without dreaming.

When I woke up, the day was well advanced. My wife had gone, but had left a note saying that she would be home for dinner at about seven. I rang the library and said I wouldn't be in.

I couldn't do anything, just wandered round from room to

room. Tidying up after my wife as I went. When she'd come home the night before she'd simply thrown off her clothes and they were still lying all over the place. Her fur coat in the hall and skirt and underclothes in the bedroom.

The papers I'd borrowed from the library were lying on the desk in the study. I didn't touch them. I started preparing the evening meal quite early.

When we were eating together that evening I didn't say a word about the nightmare, and nor did she. We just chatted superficially about everyday things. Not until later, as we sat over our coffee, did I begin to talk properly.

I told her about what I'd been reading the previous night. I gave her a detailed account of everything the documents had disclosed and the characters that inhabited them. When I'd finished, she looked at me pensively before she spoke.

It was not the documents themselves that caused her concern, but me. She was worried. She felt I ought to take some time off from all these old manuscripts, she thought I was overworking. I buried myself so deep in historical documents that I almost lived my life through them. It couldn't be healthy.

"You should go out more with me among living people," she said.

I didn't reply to that. In re-telling the story I had gone back among the figures from the past. Only now did I mention the dagger; did she think it had been retrieved?

She shrugged her shoulders.

The next day was a Thursday. Once more I stayed at home, and immersed myself in the old papers, going through the text again line by line in an attempt to understand it more fully. As usual I took notes as I read. One by one the characters came to life for me. What had happened to them, what had been their fate?

The file of documents didn't provide any answer. I had

gleaned from them all there was to be known. Except for the question of the dagger – had it been recovered, or was it still lying in the gap between the two blocks of stone?

My wife was a regular churchgoer; she went to Mass every Sunday and to confession every Thursday. I belong to the Church myself, but only very passively. However, I do occasionally go with her to Mass.

That Thursday I also accompanied her when she went to confession. I could see that she didn't like it, but she didn't say anything.

I stayed sitting on a pew in the almost empty church while she went into the confessional. As I sat in the semi-darkness something very strange happened. There was a shaft of light shining down on to the altar from the high window. I could see the figure of a woman up there, immobile, with a child in her arms.

I stared at her in terror. She was dressed in black; it was the same woman who had called to me from the jetty in my dream. Her face was turned away, and I couldn't see her features. She was there only for an instant, and then she disappeared. At that moment my wife came back, accompanied by the priest, who greeted me warmly. Again I felt that she disliked the situation, standing between her Father Confessor and her husband in the church aisle.

That same evening I began to study the maps, where I had one known point: Singing Valley. I tried to sketch in the storyteller's route, the one he followed after stabbing the poor boy in his blind rage.

It seemed clear to me that he must have come from a town on the Mediterranean coast, probably La Spezia, and that he had travelled through Singing Valley and on along the tracks until he came out on the road to Prato. From there he must have journeyed eastwards until he ended up in a town on the Adriatic coast, perhaps near Rimini. The mountains in that area extend down to the shore. That would also accord with Mary's instruction to the artist, that he should sail in the blue ship southwards to Ancona.

The next day I told my wife of my plans. I had to find the fountain. Until then, I wouldn't feel that the story had been completed and that I could put the matter out of my head.

She disapproved; she thought I should stop delving further into it now. She could see that it wasn't doing me any good. There was no chance of her coming; the business was absorbing all her time and she had already taken her holiday.

I stood my ground. I had to investigate this last lead. It wouldn't take me more than three or four days to make the trip there and back again. And I had enough holiday still to come. At that, she suddenly changed tack completely. It would certainly be good for me to have a break for a few days, perhaps even a week, and it would enable me to get the story off my mind once and for all.

Now it was she who was urging me to make the journey, and telling me I should get away as soon as possible. So I set out early on Saturday morning on the first three hundred miles to La Spezia. She got up and ate breakfast with me before I left. She had no particular plans for the weekend and was pleased just to be able to relax after a tiring week. She had been remarkably keen to get rid of me, I thought as I drove out of Rome.

I had also decided to take things easy. I drove along the coast road at a moderate speed. It was beautiful autumn weather, and a pleasant temperature. I wound down the window and enjoyed the warm breeze from the sea. When I was a good halfway to my destination I stopped for the night in a country village and put up at an inn.

I went for a long walk on the beach before dinner. The sea was perfectly still, without a ripple, and the sun was shining. Nevertheless a shiver went down my spine. I've always been afraid of the sea.

One of the few clear memories I have of my mother is of a trip to the sea. It was in 1943, the last summer of her life, when I was seven. We went for a walk along the beach one day. The sun was shining, but there was a strong wind blowing, whipping up the sea and throwing the waves right across the beach. I was frightened, but my mother comforted me.

Suddenly we saw a rainbow in the drops of water, clear and close. I remembered what I'd been taught at school, that it was God's promise to us. He would protect everyone. For a moment I felt secure.

Then my mother told me about the spectrum. That in reality it was the light that was broken up through the droplets of water and that the colours in the light had different angles of refraction, red smallest and violet greatest. That was why the rainbow appeared.

In reality. The physical fact robbed me of my feeling of security. I didn't understand the explanation, but I knew it was true. That very fact created an insurmountable distance between myself and the inexplicable, the essence of the rainbow.

The inexplicable is a necessity of life. I go deaf when someone tries to tell me about DNA molecules. I'm aware that nowadays we know how life is formed. But the person who doesn't understand the explanation and yet at the same time knows it to be true has a desert of facts between himself and the miracle. Between himself and a miracle, which, in contrast to a fact, is a necessity for living.

Only a person who is not impeded by this distance can understand love and accept it without question.

In October of that year my mother died. She was eating fish when Badoglio's voice came over the radio declaring war on Germany. She caught a bone in her throat and slowly turned blue. I sat and watched her without being able to move.

It was the Church that took care of me; I had no relatives except my mother.

Back at the inn I phoned my wife before I sat down to table. It rang for ages without an answer. But I didn't hang up; I let it go on ringing. And suddenly she answered. She sounded rather confused and almost frightened. She had lain down to rest and had fallen into a deep sleep, she said.

I arrived in La Spezia early in the afternoon of the next day. Once again I found an inn, before going out into the town on my search. In his notes the storyteller had mentioned the square in front of the church. That had to be where the fountain was situated. It wasn't difficult to find the church. It was in an old part of town, and the tower rose well above the roofs of the secular buildings around it.

I reached it in some excitement and walked across the marketplace. I looked around in disappointment. There wasn't a trace of a fountain. I asked several passers-by. They all shook their heads. No one had heard of an old fountain in that square. I walked about in the town for another hour or two, but with dwindling hope of the streets opening out into another old square with a fountain.

I discovered the municipal library, but it was closed. I recalled in annoyance that it was Sunday.

This time my wife picked up the receiver the moment I'd finished dialling the number; it was almost as if she'd stayed sitting there by the telephone.

The next morning I was at the library as soon as it opened. A very friendly librarian listened to my enquiry, that I was trying to identify a town with an ancient fountain in a square, a town that must be somewhere near the narrow path to Singing Valley. She fetched local maps of the district, showing the track to the hidden valley.

She obviously had good analytical abilities, since she studied the maps methodically and ascertained that we couldn't be talking of more than two little towns in the vicinity of La Spezia: Cibiana or Marina di Carrara.

She hadn't been living very long in the area herself, so she had never been to either of the two. But that didn't mean that she couldn't find out something about them, she assured me, and started looking out books on Ligurian topography.

By midday we'd found it. The librarian was as pleased as I was, and rather proud, when she held up a book with a picture of the old fountain in Cibiana.

According to the book it was already there in Roman times, and had a large rectangular stone-block pediment. The blocks were laid to form steps on each side up to the fountain itself. The librarian gladly supplied me with a photocopy of the picture.

I got into the car with a beating heart and drove off to Cibiana. It didn't take more than half an hour once I'd got out of the city traffic of La Spezia.

Cibiana is quite a small town, and the church and the old square are easily visible as you drive in.

I was able to park the car on the square, and quickly walked the last few steps over to the fountain, where the storyteller all those hundreds of years ago had struck down the young boy in his frenzy.

I took my bearings from the sun to locate the steps on the eastern side. There was no doubt that I was in the right place.

It was in the middle of the afternoon and the square was quite crowded. I would wait till darkness fell before I investigated more closely.

I sat down on one of the steps of the fountain.

Then it occurred to me: it was here, of course, on this very marketplace that I had just walked across, that the young woman had stripped naked for her beloved to prove her love.

This must also have been the town that witnessed the rise and fall of the weatherman.

With my pulses throbbing again I stood up and walked

slowly round the marketplace trying to conjure up the events of the past. The square was paved with huge slabs. I looked about me. Which of the streets leading off it had the young couple chosen when he led her off in his nakedness? I took one of them.

I returned to the marketplace at sunset. I could see the mountains in the east over the rooftops. In the west the sun was slowly sinking into the sea. There was a velvety half-light over the square and the town, soon followed by pitch darkness.

Now there were only one or two solitary individuals hurrying across the square on their way home. I could safely approach the crack in the steps and put my arm in without being seen. My heart was hammering in my breast as I felt carefully around inside the cavity.

There was something there. In my agitation I let it slip just as I was about to grasp it between my fingers.

A spasm of cramp seized my arm, so I pulled it out and shook it. Then I inserted my hand once again. Cautiously, very cautiously, I groped for the object in the dark narrow recess. Eager as I was, I had to take care not to push it further in.

I managed to get my index finger and middle finger round it and began to draw it slowly towards me. It moved. Twice I lost my grip. But now that it had come forward in the gap it was easier to keep a tight hold on it.

Then suddenly I was sitting with it in my hand. There was no doubt. It was an ancient dagger. The dagger.

The handle was well preserved, with beautiful inlaid stones. I weighed it solemnly in my hand. No one had touched it since the night the murder took place.

So did the storyteller not come home? Or had he abandoned the idea of retrieving it, and hastened straight to his wife instead?

Elated, I sat holding the knife, turning it over and over.

It came to me again, that strange feeling of being close to those people from long ago. I looked up and gave a shudder. In the darkness I could just make out a thickset man with near-white hair coming slowly across the square. He stopped at the foot of the steps and looked at me. He was wearing simple black clothes. His face was lined, but not old. I could see that he was moving his lips as if he was saying something to me, but I couldn't hear a sound.

I stood up, and without any conscious decision on my part, found myself descending the few steps to meet him. When I reached him I put out my hand to touch him.

My hand went straight through the figure. I still moved forward slowly towards him, and with a shiver felt myself walking right into his body.

I was again alone in the marketplace. But the dagger had not disappeared. I looked down in a daze at my right hand, clenched tightly round the handle.

I was trembling so much that it was difficult to unlock the car. I still had the knife firmly in my grasp as I sat in and drove off.

A few streets further on I came to an abrupt halt. I had to phone my wife. There was no answer, even though I let it ring for several minutes.

I got into the car again and drove towards Rome, still with the knife in my hand. I had to get home at once. It was nine o'clock.

After a while my hand was again seized by cramp. I had to turn in to the side and stop, and prise the dagger out of my palm. I laid it down carefully away from me on the empty front seat. It took some minutes for the cramp to release its hold so that I could drive on.

It was my misfortune that I didn't drive over the edge that night. I could so easily have done. The road was good and there wasn't much traffic, but I wasn't a very skilful driver and the recent events had thrown me off balance.

It was many hours before I reached home. As I approached Rome the traffic got heavier. Dazzled by the strong headlights of the incessant oncoming cars, I had to stop several times, as if to draw breath. Finally I pulled into the quiet street where we lived. I parked the car and looked up at the windows of the apartment. It was dark. It was two o'clock. I climbed stiffly and laboriously out of the car and stretched myself. Then I leaned over and picked up the dagger. I stared down at it, and at that instant it happened.

I was suddenly, for the first time in my life, possessed by an immense, uncontrollable rage. The last thing I remember is that I was running towards the house with the dagger clutched tight in my hand.